Signed for Him

J.R DUST

Authors Note & Important Information / Trigger Warnings

The contents within this book are very dark - significantly darker than the first instalment of the Duet. You can find the full list of Trigger Warnings on my website; however, the majority are also listed below. Please take these trigger warnings seriously. Your mental health is of the utmost importance.

The following Trigger Warnings and the 'Further Warning' does have spoilers included. If you do not have any triggers and would prefer to read on without spoilers, please feel free to avoid the following page.

Trigger Warnings -
Sexual Abuse
Sexual Coercion
Rape
Gore
Torture
Stockholm syndrome
Kidnap
Graphic violence
Psychological abuse
Child Abuse (past tense)
Physical abuse

AUTHORS NOTE & IMPORTANT INFORMATION / TRIGGER ...

Dub-Con
Non-Con
Degradation
Suicidal Thoughts
Necrophilia
Murder
Miscarriage
Self-Harm
Mental Health (depression and anxiety specifically)
Character death
This story does have an unconventional/realistic HEA (Happily Ever After)
Further Warning/Potential Spoiler -
Not all characters will make it through this story. If you feel that this puts this book in a space that isn't suited to you for any reason, please do not read on.

Similarly to real life, I feel that everyone deserves the truth - even the ugly truth as well as happiness after trauma and loss. This is something that is explored in this story.

Language Differences

I'm a UK based author that writes using British English. For anyone based and reading outside of the UK, this may mean that some phrases, words, shop names or locations seem strange or as though a mistake has been made but this isn't the case (unless it really is a mistake 😅). If you do find a mistake, feel free to send a message my way!

Recommended for readers 18 years and older.

If you ever need to contact me, please feel free to do so at j.rdust_author@yahoo.com

One

GRAY - 3 WEEKS EARLIER

"Have you checked on Charlie tonight? She's going to that party at the Clubhouse, isn't she?" I ask as he walks ahead of me. I hate that I could only watch her from a distance. At least he gets to see her, even if he does have to keep his distance. Not as though it seems he is doing a very good job at it.

This whole thing is the most fucked up situation I've ever found myself in, and I've been in some very fucking precarious situations before now, so that is seriously saying something.

"Yeah, she's got Crow and the shithead with her," he tells me.

He doesn't like Victor. I'm not exactly too keen on him myself. We knew Crow was an O'banian. Hell, I was the one that had helped him get into the Cobras to start the investigation into the club for his family so the whole merging shit could move on a bit quicker. Not as though anyone besides me and the fucker next to me knows that. Well, Crow, too, of course.

But Victor - he is a whole other issue. I don't know enough about him and I don't like that. I don't like that someone is around my sister that I haven't had the chance to fuck around with a bit to see his true colours first. I mean, I am not exactly thrilled about anyone being with my baby sister, but at least I trust Crow. I know he would do anything to protect her. It had started as an assignment, but even I saw the way they looked at each other before I left. It was the only reason I could leave and trust that she would be ok. I sigh at the thought.

Yeah, and look how that turned out, you idiot. Look at where you are now.

"What room did he say they'd be in?" I ask as we continue walking through the hallway towards the main rooms.

"197. They got a new girl in tonight. I dread to fucking think what they're doing to her. Apparently this one's into pain though, so they'll probably be ripping her up," he mutters as his face distorts in disgust.

Matt and his wannabe Danny class themselves as 'Doms'. From what I am aware of, that includes respect, consent, rules, and a safe word. None of those things are included in Matt and Danny's sex life. It is rape. Simple as that. No matter how willing girls are to come back with them, they are no longer interested when they realise they'll likely end up in hospital or - like too many of the girls I've seen carted out of here - dead. They meet girls on dating sites, claiming to be things they aren't, and then drug and drag them back to this slice of hell to ruin and rape them.

"Has Dad figured out that they're crossing him yet? Shit, even just their attitude should get them kicked out, shouldn't it?" I wonder aloud. My dad gives people too many chances. Like way too many chances.

He is a man so loyal to some stupid MC code that he doesn't even see what is right in front of him.

He had this vision of me taking over the MC after Liam is done, but I can't think of anything worse. I don't know exactly what I want to do or where I want to be in life, but running the Club and the Cobras is not it. I know that much. But then again, maybe now that I have seen this darkness I would have a better chance of taking charge and knowing a fucked up person when I meet them. There are definitely plenty of them here.

Matt and Danny had been planted into the Cobras before I left. At different times so as not to gain too much interest or query. I had no idea they were anything but your typical Class A fucking bastards until I got trapped here and he started telling me more than he should have.

Matt and Danny are lunatics. Legitimate psychopaths with no care or consideration for the women they break. They seem to think that because they don't have STIs and wear condoms most of the time that it is fine. It isn't.

And if I say anything? Charlie. Charlie is always the threat. Every single person here knows they only have to mention her name and I'll do anything they ask, and I fucking hate it.

I don't think I'd ever wished to be an only child. Even when Charlie was pissing me off as a kid or wanting to hang out with my friends when I didn't want her to, I never wished she wasn't there. But for the sake of my sanity and both of our freedoms, I wish I was an only child now, even if only so that they couldn't threaten me with her safety.

I have complete faith in Crow's ability to take care of her but then again, if you've got a bunch of twats planning and attempting to get to someone, there's only so much that one man can do.

I look to my right and find he's slowed down to match my pace. He isn't any more keen on this than I am.

It isn't exactly a friendship me and this fucker have, but while we're both stuck in a scenario we don't want to be in, we definitely trust each other more than anyone else in this shithole.

"Nope. No one likes them, but you know what your dad's like. He thinks he has to have evidence of bad behaviour to kick them out. He won't just do it because they're twats," He huffs out as we round the corner.

My head shakes of its own accord, mad at my dad for being

too trusting. Mad at myself for landing myself here. Mad at Charlie for being vulnerable and someone I care so highly for. Worst bit is, I knew my mum was in with some bad people. I knew there was a chance they'd get to me before I got to them, but what I didn't expect was to be carted off by a whole other fucking band of bastards while I was busy worrying about my mother's men.

"I swear to god, if I have to act happy when I walk in and see them carving up some poor girl again, I'm gonna lose my mind." The minute I show even an ounce of disgust at what the animals in this place do to women is the same moment they use Charlie's freedom against me. They know she is my weakness and I can't fucking stand it, but if being a prisoner here means that she is safe then I'll survive it for as long as I have to.

"Just smile and wave. They'll be going to see the boss and then we can get the girl to the doctor. Problem solved." He says it like it's so simple. I've been taught my whole life to protect women, to love and care for them.

He's so used to seeing screwed up and messed up shit that I don't think it phases him anymore. Well, no, that's a lie. It does. I know it does. I can see it in the twitch of his eye that he tries to hide every time we walk in on something gruesome or every time he's tortured and hurt as punishment for caring for Charlie, but he handles it a lot better than I do. Maybe if I'd grown up the way he had then I would too.

I'd asked him once how he managed to see the women be treated so badly and do nothing about it. He told me that you can respect women all you like but that doesn't mean that everyone else will too.

I might be gay and so the whole holding the woman and loving her thing doesn't apply, but that doesn't change the fact that I still respect fuck out of the women around me - whether I know them or not. I hate the fucked up things the men here did to the girls they take, but I can't do a thing about it without more threats to Charlie's life.

You go out on a mission to find your mother and you end up held hostage and threatened. I know how to land myself in the furnace of fuck ups, that's for sure.

"Here we go, this one," he says as he taps my back, gives me a fake smile and encourages me to do the same before opening the door and motions for me to enter first.

The smile plastered on my face doesn't falter while I greet them until I see the carnage they've created.

Fuck.

There is blood everywhere. All over them and the poor girl underneath them. Her body is red with very little sign of life. I can hardly even see her face. But that's the way they like it.

"Oh shit," Danny says as his body stops pumping into the poor fucking state of a woman underneath him. My horrified eyes drift up to Matt kneeling on the girl's arms as he slaps her again before looking up at me with fear filling his eyes.

Why does he look afraid? They're usually cocky as fuck when someone finds them in this sort of situation, happily showing off their conquests and the pain they've caused.

And that's when I look at the woman's face for the first time since they've leaned away from her and feel the instant horror and rage coat my vision.

Charlie.

My mind seems to enter a desolate state, my body unmoving as I stand wide eyed and nearly delirious with anger and shock.

Before I can convince my body to register the shock and move, the fucker beside me is on them as he lets out a monstrous roar. His hands grab the knife I hadn't noticed that was in Danny's grip. I watch on as he crouches down between them, over Charlie, and swipes his hand back and forth, stabbing them both repeatedly until they're still and nearly lifeless beside her.

"Get the fucking doctor. Now," he roars out as he picks her up gently, with utter fury in his eyes.

I thought I was saving her by doing as they said but now they have us both.

Fuck. How did this happen?

Two

CHARLIE - THE PRESENT

My whole body feels heavy. My eyelids refuse to open, despite the many attempts I make to move them. It feels like my eyelashes are fluttering from the small tickle on my face and yet nothing happens. I can feel my eyes moving, but all I see is darkness. I try to make my hand move and feel only the smallest twitch of my fingers. And that's when the pain hits. The excruciating pain that courses through my body and is unrelenting in its desire to make me wish for death. It's a burning, throbbing, stabbing pain that seems to attack every part of me.

"She's awake," I hear a shallow feminine voice say, a voice lacking any emotion or care. A voice I don't recognise, I realise.

Footsteps follow the words spoken. Three sets of footsteps. One is light, leading away from me while the two others are heavier, louder footfalls that get closer and closer to my side.

"It's time to wake up now, Chars." It's Gray. Gray's here. Why is Gray here? Where is here? Am I at home?

No. This doesn't feel like home.

What happened? Why am I in pain in a place that I don't recognise the feelings and smells of? What do I last remember? My mind draws a blank as I think of the morning I spent getting ready for the party at the Club after being to the doctor. After the time I'd spent with Victor and Crow. I recall going to the club, having vodka-

And then I remember.

The men. Waking up in a place I didn't know. The brutal assault they laid on my body. I instantly want to rip at my skin, feeling the disgust and turmoil within me wanting to claw its way out.

I feel disgusting and helpless knowing what happened to me as I wonder how I'm still alive. I am alive, aren't I? I must be, I heard Gray.

Am I in the hospital? But no, I realise, I can't be. There would be doctors and nurses that would be surrounding me in a hospital.

I think back to Gray. Gray is here. The same Gray that I haven't seen for a lifetime. They greeted Gray like a friend, not an enemy, I suddenly remember. Where are we?

I subconsciously twitch the moment Gray's warm hands connect with mine, my eyes shooting open at the contact - my eyes connecting with his.

I can feel the fear he must see in my face. I don't want to be here. Wherever here is. I want to be at home. I want to cry and scream and ask the world why I deserved this, but before I even open my mouth, my body hits me with the most excruciating pain I've ever felt. Except it's not in one place. There's not a single hit of pain. It's everywhere. Every wire and line within my body feels like it's on fire.

"It hurts," I cry out quietly to Gray, my voice barely more than a whisper as tears escape and run down my cheeks.

His eyes fill with sorrow as he looks down at me with his eyebrows crammed together.

"I'm so fucking sorry, Chars. I'm so fucking sorry," he tells me as he places his head in my hand.

I watch in utter confusion, the pain ebbing to the background as I look around and try to work out my surroundings and why I'm here. Why I'm not home in my bed.

I just want to go home. The anxiety in my stomach rolls and shifts, waves of nausea hitting me at the uncomfort. Not just the physical discomfort but the idea that I have no idea what is going on or why I'm not where I'm meant to be.

It is a hospital room, though I don't feel that I'm in a hospital. I'm not sure why, but I'm certain I'm not safe. I don't feel like I'll ever feel safe again.

As my head slowly turns, looking around the room, my eyes connect with a monster. Not a new one but one that does make the fear that lingers rise to the surface.

I spent so many years looking up to him, thinking that he would be my saviour, my family forever and yet the last time I spoke to him, I knew. I knew there was a deeper and darker part to his soul than I had ever realised or wished to see.

"I'm not going to hurt you," he says as he takes a few tentative steps closer to me. His presence is as overpowering and outrageous now as it ever had been and when I'm feeling most vulnerable, it terrifies me.

"What's happening? Where am I? Why are you here? Where's Dad? And Crow? And Victor?" I ask, my throat dry and my voice hoarse. I feel the tears rising to the surface, though I do my best to blink and blink, to make them go away.

Make them go away.

"Please take me home." I turn to Gray, unsure that I can trust him but knowing that I hold more trust in my brother than in the monster on my other side.

Gray dabs at his eyes as he lifts his face, his eyes still filled with a mixture of guilt and remorse as he shakes his head at me.

"I can't leave, let alone take you home," he tells me sadly.

I fight through the pain consuming my body, shifting so that I'm sat up in the bed, pulling the blanket with me to cover the hospital nightgown underneath.

Who changed me out of the clothes I was in? Who saw the

damage that I knew was done to my body? I didn't need to see myself; I could feel the bruising and stiffness in my very bones to know that I was inexplicably and fatally changed.

"Why can't you leave?" I ask him, my eyes alternating between him and the monster beside me, unwilling to turn my back on him for the fear of what he may do.

"They promised that if I stayed, they wouldn't hurt you. They wouldn't take you but now that they have you, if I try to leave or help you leave, they'll hurt you even more," he wrenches out, his face looking like he's about to sob in my lap at any given moment.

I think through what he's said. They? Who are they? The same they from the letter he left me? Just sitting up in the stiff bed has my body and muscles aching, I'm certain I don't have the energy to escape, let alone ask the questions I want to right now.

"Can you take me home?" I ask quietly as I turn to Liam. The monster. No doubt the devil behind all of this.

He watches me, his eyes filled with nothing but darkness.

"I can't. I can demand that you're mine though. No one else will hurt you then."

A laugh gurgles through my dry throat, a sound that resembles a choked sigh more than the sarcastic laugh that was intended.

"Right. Then only you could hurt me," I say.

I'm trapped. One way or another, whichever way I go, I'm trapped. I can't move. I can't leave. I can't get off this bed. There are monsters everywhere. I want to curl up in a ball, close my eyes, and not open them again until I'm in the arms of safety. Until this is all over and someone wakes me from this nightmare, telling me that none of it was real, that everything will be OK, but I'm not sure that anything will ever be ok again.

I want Crow. Despite my care for Victor, it's not him I crave. I want Crow's warmth, his laughter, his reassuring smile. I want his arms around me and his voice whispering in my ear, telling me that everything will be OK. I want him to hug me and hold me and carry me home.

"I'll take care of you. I may be the villain in your story but I promise you, I won't hurt you."

I inwardly cringe at the statement, the irony of his insistence on keeping me uninjured when I'm sitting in a hospital bed feeling more physically and mentally drained than I ever have in my life.

I had been hurt in every way before from different things, whether that be illness or heartbreak; from those I love dying or leaving; and yet the pain I'm in now doesn't even come close to comparing. It's a situation I never envisioned being in and one that everyone warned me of. You never think it will happen to you until it does, that's the saying, right? I can't count how many times I was told that when I was younger when Nina, my best friend, and I wanted to go out alone.

Liam looks at me with a hint of what looks to be shame or remorse in his eyes, but I dismiss the notion that he could possibly feel bad for this situation or for me when I have no doubt he was at least a part of the reason I'm here.

"How long have I been asleep?" I ask Gray, not wanting to spend any more time than necessary looking at Liam's face or thinking about the implications of what I assume he's done.

"The doctor put you into an induced coma to let your body heal. You've been out for just over three weeks," he tells me, his voice gentle and hushed.

Three weeks.

My God, three weeks.

"Why haven't they found me?" I rasp out. I want to cry. I can feel my chest filling with emotion. If I've been gone for three weeks and they haven't found me, who's to say that they ever will? They have so many resources at their disposal and if they haven't found me yet, I dread the idea that they won't at all.

As I shift further up the bed, pulling the thin, crisp sheet along with me, Gray and Liam look at one another, a silent conversation passing between them. Gray's face looks even more grim now than it did moments ago.

"What happened? Oh god, please tell me they're ok," I demand, knowing for certain that I couldn't handle the idea of anything bad happening to any of those that I care for. I would rather they didn't find me at all than get hurt in the process of trying to get to me.

"This place is well covered. Hidden. It's unlikely that they will find you. The boss has spent years making sure that this place is impossible to find. They're fine. No one is hurt outside of you," Liam says as he moves to sit on the chair next to the bed on my left.

My mind doesn't seem to know how to comprehend what I'm being told. Nothing and nowhere is impossible to find. They will find me. I just have to wait. I just have to wait for a little while and they'll find me, I tell myself. The comfort I attempt to bring to my mind is pointless though. I know that the first twenty-four hours after a disappearance are the most important - the most likely time for a victim of kidnapping to be found and if after three weeks I haven't been found, it's unlikely that I will be.

Not impossible though. Not impossible. Even if I have to find a way to get out of here myself, I will. I just need to be patient. There is always a weakness, I just need to find it.

"I want to get up. I need to go to the bathroom. I want to shower." The truth is that I want a moment alone to cry my heart out and repair it before I have to face Liam again, but I'm not going to say that.

"I'll give you a hand, come here," Gray says as he helps me up from the bed and holds onto my arm as I walk on unsteady and jelly-like legs to a door on the opposite side of the room.

He walks me inside and shows me where everything is, telling me that he'll be just outside if I need him. There isn't a window or an accessible vent. No way out aside from the door that will lead back to Gray and Liam. I can't face leaving without Gray anyway, and I'm not sure my body has the resources to do much escaping right now as it is.

I turn on the shower and step inside, hating the new scars surrounding my body from the assault but lapping up the warm water on my skin like heaven and hell. My skin feels so sensitive to the pellets of water being thrown its way, but the warmth engulfs me. My mind races at the conundrum I find myself in, but I cut off the thoughts abruptly, knowing that if I start crying alone, I'll probably never stop. I throw my head back under the cascade of liquid and wash myself quickly before stepping out and drying myself off.

"I've got some clothes here for you. Open the door a little and I'll hand them to you," Gray says. I do as he says and grab hold of the clothes.

Once dressed, I find the mirror above the sink and stare horrified at the face in front of me. Tears brim to the surface as I look on at the woman staring back at me. That's not me. It can't be. But it is. My hands lift and the woman in the mirror copies, tracing my fingers over the monstrous scar still healing over my face. I remember them cutting me. Hurting me. I thought I was going to die, but it isn't until this moment when I look in the mirror that I realise how truly broken I look. There are dark circles under my eyes, nearly healed bruises over the top of my body that are visible even with the clothes on.

I always thought that scars weren't a big issue but now that I have one running down my face, I want to break and cry and scream at the prospect of never looking the same again because having physical scars means that it isn't just my body that will never feel the same, but my mind too, and while stuck in this furnace of hell, I have no idea how I'm supposed to recoup. I have no idea who to trust or how much.

Three

CHARLIE

My backside throbs and burns as he pulls the whip back again, my body convulsing over the table, shivers running through me as I await the continued physical assault that lashes through my senses.

My fingernails dig into the side of the table, the pain tremendous as splinters from the wood embed themselves into my skin, but it's serving as the only distraction I can find. I hear the sound of the whip flying through the air towards my backside once more with a guttural roar filling the room as the cold material smacks against my uncovered skin, causing another twitch of my body, another sob. I do everything I can to hold it in as my head shakes of its own accord, the tears spilling onto my cheeks and the table below me as I try to stop myself from wailing out in pain.

"What number is that?" Liam rasps out, his breaths as harsh as mine are as he pants and takes a moment's respite.

"Twelve." My voice is barely above a whisper as he rounds the table and crouches down to meet my eyes, lifting my head by my hair in his hand as he does.

"How many? I couldn't hear you," he asks again, his voice

steady as I watch his chest through my blurry vision, my eyes filled with tears.

"Twelve," I mutter quietly, acid and bile filling my mouth as I speak.

I don't want to be here. I want to go home. It's the only thought that occupies my mind - the only thought that I allow to keep me company. The thought of Crow pulls me through the depressive daze I find myself nearly submitting to daily.

Liam places my head back down on the table, my cheek on the cold wood beneath it. He strokes my hair as he takes a deep breath, "Do you need more or is that enough?"

"That's enough." I give in.

There's no point fighting it. I've been fighting it since I first entered this apartment. Fighting him, fighting the inevitable that I knew would end up happening if I wasn't found soon enough. I just hoped I would be found before I lost the strength I needed to keep fighting. But it's too late. I can't keep going - not mentally nor physically.

"I'm not doing this because I want to hurt you, I'm doing this because I don't want you hurt," he emphasises as he rounds the table, reaching the back of me as his hands begin roaming along the back of my bare thighs.

He made me strip, so that I was in nothing but my bra before he punished me. It wasn't unusual but that didn't mean that it was any less cruel. It is humiliating being covered in scars. I hate it, but to have to bare them to someone unwillingly makes it so much worse.

The punishment doesn't usually go on this long, but I think he sensed how close I was to breaking, how little fight I had left in me. He knew that he just had to go that little bit further before I surrendered.

His hands are wet, likely covered in my blood and sweat as they draw closer and closer to my entrance. The feeling of anyone, let alone him, being that close to the intimate parts of me makes me want to be sick, but I know that will cause me more pain so I hold back the urge and wait, unmoving as he does as he pleases with the body that is barely mine anymore.

He can do what he wants to the shell of me. He insists that he is doing it to protect me, but the notion seems as laughable as it is improbable.

"It's me or them and despite what you may think, I'm the better choice. They would take it in turns with you, pass you around their friends, take you without any preparation, do whatever they wanted with you. At least here, at least now, it's just you and me." And it was that thought that makes me shiver, that makes my body shake uncontrollably rather than the hands and fingers that are caressing my folds.

Though I'm sure he takes pleasure in feeling my body shake, assuming that he is the cause through pleasure rather than sickness at the idea of it being just me and him.

I understand but that doesn't mean that I believe him entirely. Gray had told me that what he was saying was true - that the other men here had declared that if he didn't use me then they would, and from the stories Gray had told me of what transpired outside of this apartment, I have no doubt that I don't want to be a part of that. I know that in his own mind, Liam feels he is the better option, but that doesn't change the fact that I am certain he is happy about it and that was why I fought it.

Despite the fact that I hate it, it isn't because he is unattractive, it isn't because I can't let him do it, nor is it because I hadn't ever thought about it because I had. It is because I feel like every time he touches me, I am cheating on Crow. I have no idea why Crow over Victor is the deciding factor. I adore Victor, but the more time I spend away from him, the more I realise that I only miss him in the way that I miss Nina or Alice, not in the way that I miss Crow. When I sob into my pillow next to a sleeping Liam at night, it is Crow's touch I crave, his words, his hushed whispers. Him.

Liam's heavy breathing stops my thoughts where they are, erasing any thoughts of those on the outside from my mind.

I knew what the options were and I didn't want either one. He'd repeatedly told me that he was being threatened, that he didn't have a choice. I knew that, but that didn't change the fact that I still didn't want it. I wanted to be saved. I wanted the torture and punishment to go on for as long as it could before I had to finally give in so that I could be saved before that time occurred, but I can't take anymore.

The thing I hate, probably more than him touching me, is the fact that him touching me makes my insides warm and my core wet. I hate that my body seemed so willing and pliant as he touched me for the first time. The last time I was touched there, it was taken from me so violently that I never wanted to be touched again and yet through his touch, my body seemed intent on not only surviving that but on enjoying it orgasming again.

The hand not on my core's entrance flicks and rubs at my clit, my body responding tenfold despite my attempts to stay as still as possible. The friction he is creating has me arching my body and biting down on my palm to cover the cries that threaten to spill free.

"You're so wet, my baby girl, you're so responsive to my touch." His voice is molten, like lava as his words do nothing but set alight my body once more. I hate this. Mentally, I hate it. I want his hands off me, I want to go home, I want to cry and wash his touch away and never be near him again but he is right, my body seems to adore his touch. My abdomen feels more and more full as his finger gently slips inside of me, his other hand rubbing against me between my folds, the pressure building higher and higher until I feel the one thing I dread. I dread it because he knows. He knows that my body isn't against him as much as my mind is, and that brings the sobs forward the moment I feel the tightened orgasm release all over his hand as his fist pumps slow down before he finally takes his finger out of me and pulls his hand away, the cold air suddenly making my body shiver again.

His hands reach around my waist and lifts me to my feet, my legs wobbling, my backside still throbbing from the pain that, although not nearly as bad, is certainly not diminished. My core throbs as violently as my backside does, coming down from the most horrendous and yet mind-blowing orgasm.

His breath falls down on my hair, his head above mine as he turns me towards him, my eyes downcast, unwilling and not wanting to look at the man and monster in front of me.

He leads me to the bathroom, my body aching and burning with the aftermath of both the pleasure and pain that he forced upon me.

"Stand there. Don't move." I don't acknowledge that he's spoken, nor do I disobey. My body feels numb and tingly outside of the pain, wondering why it was so easy for him to get me to a place of lust filling my gaze even through the pain.

I feel like I've cheated on Crow, despite logically knowing that he would want me to do whatever I could to stay alive and well, and yet I don't feel either of those things. I'm surviving, sure, but it feels endless, this cycle with him, and the longer we spend together, the more I can feel the brick hard barrier I had put up crumbling at his feet. He knows it as well as I do, and that kills me.

I care for him in ways I hate admitting. After spending so many years with him as part of my family, I know there's good within him, even if I feel like I haven't seen any of it for aeons. I wonder if he faked it but realise that he surely couldn't have. He used to care for me, genuinely, with a ferocity that I admired as a child and a teenager and yet, as I stand here now, I question what changed and how it occurred. Was he always this way and I just didn't see it because I was looking at him through the eyes of an adoring child?

Liam interrupts my fraying thoughts with a flannel in his hands, him on his knees in front of me as he gently rubs the cloth across my thighs and my outer legs; over and over again he puts the flannel under the warm water and returns it to me, to my skin, cleaning the blood, sweat and remnants of the orgasm away as I stand unmoving.

There's something sensual about his movements, about this vulnerability and the silence with no words spoken. Something strange. He washes me delicately, as if I'm a vase that could break at any moment. Maybe if he had been this gentle with me from the start it would have been easier for me to give in. Not that I should, but maybe I could have. I could have even wanted to.

When he's finished and uses the towel to dry my naked and marred skin, he pulls his fluffy robe around me, taking me to the bedroom and laying me on my stomach on top of the mattress. My hands find themselves attached underneath the pillow as I lay my head upon it. I'm not sure what he's expecting from me, and a small part of me dreads that he'll come onto me again, but as he kneels by the side of my head and looks into my eyes, I see only hurt and despair. This is the man I knew as a child. The one that was caring and thoughtful, the one that didn't want me injured. Ever. Unless it was by his hands apparently.

"You're going to rest," he tells me as he pushes a strand of my hair from in front of my eyes backward. I don't respond, watching silently as he eyes me curiously.

He leans down, his lips finding my forehead as he plants a kiss upon my skin.

"Sleep, my beautiful girl. I'll read." I fight the urge to do just that, but I feel my eyes closing of their own accord as his voice reads the words that lull me to sleep and his fingers comb through my hair.

Four

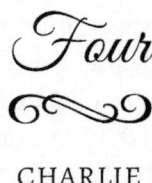

CHARLIE

"Do you think I could see Gray again soon?" I ask, adjusting my voice to sound as sweet as I can possibly make it without Liam noticing how fake I'm being.

Five hours and all hell is going to break loose. Five hours and I'm going to be saved.

I hope.

Liam was right when he made that promise to me while I was in the hospital bed, wishing for death to take me home if no one else could. Well, right to an extent. He could protect me from everyone else. He hasn't let anyone near me besides from himself and Gray since I've been here but that also means, exactly as I had suspected, that it is him I found myself subjected to instead--and the strangest part about that? Liam is a completely different man to the one I thought he was. I mean, no surprise there, and I do not mean that in a positive way.

I had known from my conversations with Crow and from Gray's letter that he wasn't as he seemed, but even then I don't think I knew or even suspected how mentally unhinged he was. I'm not sure if he acted sane or at least partially so because he knew he needed to or if something had happened that had changed him, because this man in front of me is a completely different character to the one I knew as a child.

His eyes lift, meeting mine from across the table. The very same table he bent me over while he whipped me and made me cum. God, even thinking about it makes my stomach twist and my mind revolt. I hate how easily he can sway my body.

He watches me as he chews his food. The food I made, like the perfectly capable housewife he wants me to be. So I do, I act amazingly. I'd never been interested in drama or the theatre classes in school, but my gosh, have I put on the largest and most deceitful act of my life since being in his presence. If being what he wants me to be allows me to be hurt only by him then I can cope with that. I would prefer to be hurt by only him, even over and over again, than to be tortured and tormented by the animals I have caught glances and whispers of in the hallways.

Gray has told me of the barbaric things that go on outside of the confines of Liam's apartment, and as much as I hate being a prisoner and hurt by him, it is preferable than being treated even worse by those outside the door that holds me here.

"I'm not sure you seeing him so regularly is a good thing. He acts out after he's seen you, and you give me more attitude too. I'm not sure I like it," he tells me, his lips lifting into a smirk that he knows will goad me. He does this on purpose - tries to antagonise me so that I say something he doesn't like or act aggressively and then enjoys punishing me for it.

Five hours and he won't be in charge of me anymore. I just need to make sure he doesn't know that.

Despite my initial reservations about giving in to him, I knew I had to. It was the only way to live here. I spent my first few days out of the hospital in this apartment with him, with the occasional visit from Gray when he was allowed to see me. I also spent the first few days telling Liam exactly what I thought in between my crying fits and outbursts of anger - until he snapped. I had since decided that I would be smart. Wise. Use the brain that my father had raised me with and be exactly what

Liam wanted until I found a way to get myself and Gray away from here.

The strong, independent and stubborn part of me hated it but it was the safest way to live.

I had just about given up on the hope of being rescued. I had no doubt in my mind that my father, Crow, Victor, and both clubs would have been looking for me, but wherever I am must be far enough away and so far off the radar that they can't find me, or else I wouldn't still be in this hellhole. Assuming that Gray's plan works though, I can be out of here tonight.

"What if I promise to be good? And I'll make sure that Gray doesn't act out anymore either. You know how hard I've been trying," I insist as I look at him once more, masking the frustration and anger I wish I could unleash without consequence.

Liam hums for a moment, twisting his fork over and over in his hand before placing it down on his plate and looking at me with a triumphant grin.

"I tell you what, how about we go to the bedroom and if you're a good girl, I'll let Gray come and see you later when I go to work." I can feel the bile rising up my throat, but I fight to hold it down.

I thought the pain would be the worst form of torture he would put me through while being in this cage, but I was wrong. So wrong. Within hours of returning from the hospital room after his first beating of me, he insisted that I kiss him. To show him how sorry I was. Within a week, he insisted that I hug him, to show my care and gratitude. A few days later, he whipped me, making me promise to always call him Daddy or Master when he forced himself inside of or on top of me. As if my body hadn't been through enough. As if my mind could handle anymore forms of torture. I didn't always give in to begin with. I fought. Hard - and ended up once again covered in bruises and cuts. So now I do give in.

I'm not someone that enjoys pain, or someone that is good with pain. I remember hearing stories from the Cobras wives about how well they had handled the pain in childbirth, how high their pain threshold was. Mine is not. I am terrible with pain and I can't claim otherwise. Between the mental and physical torture of being here, the forced orgasms are the better option.

Liam stands from his chair, the scraping of the wooden chair on the tiled floor sending shivers through me as he tucks it back in and begins his walk to me, his hand out, waiting for mine to be placed over top of his.

Five hours and this won't be my life anymore.

I lift my unsteady body up and place my hand in his calloused one, feeling revolted at even our hands touching - in part because I'm not at all revolted. His warmth and his soft touches do things to my body that I despise.

I always used to think holding hands was such a romantic gesture and now the only thing romantic about my life is the overwhelming sadness when I wake from a dream filled with Crow.

I close my eyes, willing away any thoughts of him or anyone else outside of this place, knowing it will only make this next part harder as he pulls me along to the bedroom.

So much of why I hate it is because I don't. I don't hate it at all and that guts me more than anything else. The first few times I pleasured him, I ran to the bathroom to be sick as soon as he left, but the longer it goes on, the more I've learned how to push the right buttons with him, how to get my way without him knowing that I'm doing it.

I've learnt a lot - one of the newest things I've learnt is that Liam is very capable sexually. Although I would much prefer I didn't have to do it, to give in to him, the fact that he insists on making me have an orgasm daily kills me because every single time, it makes me feel like I am losing my sanity. Losing my sanity because my body adores his touch while my mind will do anything to get rid of it. And the longer I'm away from Victor and Crow, the more I start to wonder if it might be easier to let the submissive, vulnerable, darker side of me learn to care for Liam. But now Gray has a plan.

Five hours.

I feel like my whole mindset is altering every day, every time he touches me or becomes tender with me.

"Strip for me, baby girl. Let me see what's mine," he whispers in my ear as we enter his bedroom.

I waste no time, immediately taking off the dress covering my body and placing it on the nightstand on my side of the bed. I'm left with a slight chill, wearing only my bra and underwear. Ones that Liam picked out, of course. I keep my eyes downcast, gazing at the cream carpet - just how he likes it.

"Now get on your knees, baby. Show your master how good you can be," he demands, the lust already filling his voice, thickening it if possible.

I take a step closer to him and fall to my knees, waiting while he strips himself of the clothes he's wearing.

It's so strange to be in such a fucked up routine. To know what I'm meant to do and yet somehow, knowing gives me comfort. I know what I can and can't do now. I know what makes him angry. I know what pleases him and until the moment I'm out of this place, pleasing him keeps me from being hurt. Pleasing him pleases me in the most screwed up way. The sounds he makes when I turn him on fuels me to do it even more.

His length bobs in front of me, already fully erect as his hands grasp my hair, forcing my head forward until his length takes residence inside of my mouth.

I move my head rhythmically back and forth, sucking and licking at the muscle in my mouth as Liam rocks his hips into me further. His moans fill the air around me. My eyes water incessantly as he pushes his cock to the back of my throat, choking me on it.

"You're such a good girl, aren't you?" he asks as he juts

forward once more before pulling his cock from my mouth, signalling for me to move to the bed.

I lay on my back on the bed, exactly as he likes, as he stands at the base and watches me with a smile on his face.

"Take your bra and panties off for me. Daddy wants to treat his little girl," he tells me, unmoving, watching me as I hastily do as I'm told.

I can handle the whole 'master' thing. I hate admitting it, but it turns me on as much as it seems to turn him on, but it's when he refers to himself as Daddy that I cringe.

"Now open your legs for me."

The cold air brushes along my core as I do, my eyes not moving from him, taking my cues on what to do from his every move.

"So fucking perfect," he mutters as he pulls me by my ankles to the bottom of the bed so that my core is mere centimetres from his face.

He lifts my legs over his shoulders before spreading my lips with his fingers, his tongue lapping up the space over my bead with haste and greed. The sensation and friction from his tongue and stubble has my body arching from the bed, my legs tightening around him. He has me melting and moaning in seconds.

His hands move to my waist, holding me in place as he laps up the inside of me, his tongue darting in and out of my body while his fingers squeeze my sides. The mixture of pleasure and pain has an involuntary groan leaving my lips, much to Liam's pleasure, his dark chuckle surrounding me.

My hips move of their own accord, desperate for more, to be closer to the tongue and face between my legs. My insides cramp and pulse as he crams his tongue into me and over my bud continually, lifting me higher, closer and closer to release.

He's done it so many times now that he knows exactly how to get me there. How to make my body writhe for him and his touch.

His hands climb down from my hips to my thighs, pushing my legs apart until it's painful, his tongue not once halting in its assault of my core.

His face lifts, his eyes finding mine, his smirk and my pleasure coating his face, making it glisten.

"You're going to cum on my tongue like a good girl now, Charlie. Do you understand?"

I nod. Yes.

"Tell me. Say the words." My body moves closer, desperate for the friction.

"Yes," I whimper out, the words tasting bitter in my mouth as I do.

Yes what?"

"Yes, Master." I close my eyes as I speak, hating the way it affects me.

He smiles once more at me as I open my eyes again before bolting back down to take what's his, his tongue flicking desperately along my clit while his fingers enter me, thrusting in and out continually as I grow closer to the release he wants.

A whimper and a groan escape me as my hands find their way to his hair, pushing his head closer, torturously closer, the friction and need of him overwhelming as I claw at him, my legs tightening around him as my pussy pulses and releases the orgasm it was dying for.

My breathing calms, my body sated as he lifts his naked body on top of my own.

"You're such a good girl for me. Well done. Now it's time to ruin you and fill you up," he tells me, his voice thick with need and lust as his length slips over my entrance, teasing my body as my hips lift to him, taking the tip without permission.

His constant want to impregnate me terrifies every part of my soul - for more reasons than I can even begin to count. I was on the contraceptive injection, which lasts three months. I know I've been here for over a month, but I lost track of the days eventually, meaning that I now have no idea if the one thing inside of my body meant to protect me still will.

He chuckles heartily with his hands beside my head, his lips on my arched neck.

"So desperate for this cock, aren't you, my greedy girl." His lips catch mine in a dangerously rare kiss, the taste of myself on his tongue filling my mouth.

It's at that moment that his length fills me, a gasp leaving my lips, straight into his as his thick dick penetrates me and every part of my body that counts.

His jagged breath beats over my mouth as he thrusts in and out of me in quick succession, my hips meeting his every thrust, my body being unaware of how bad this man truly is. My body adores him and his touch, even when my mind knows it shouldn't. But in moments like these, moments when he takes me, it's easier to let him, to allow it and to force the logical side of me that wants to fight my want and need for him to be quiet. Any time I've fought this it only ended up in more pain. A pain that I won't ever feel again if I can get past tonight.

His hands come to my throat, squeezing and ebbing away at it as my vision darkens and my lungs begin to struggle. Not long now. When he grabs my neck, I know it's not long. The pleasure filling my body intensifies, seemingly in awe of the pain and pressure he puts on me, a second orgasm only a few thrusts away as he consumes my body.

His juts become rabid, his groans immeasurable and his hands tighter around my neck as his seed fills me, my pussy clinging to his cock in bursts as my own orgasm wraps around him.

My body relaxes at the same time that his does, his head nestling between my shoulder and neck, his chest and stomach landing directly above mine as he puts his weight on top of me.

"You're such a good girl for me," he whispers in my ear as my eyes begin to flutter closed, the daylight from the window ebbing away as the sun hides for the evening.

"Come here," he tells me as he lifts his sticky, sweat-covered body from mine and lies beside me, his arm out above my head. An invitation to curl up beside him. I check the clock as I do, my heart hammering in my chest so hard I'm terrified that he'll feel it. Four hours. Four hours until I can go home.

My body fits next to his disgustingly well, the touch of his body moulded to my own bringing me more comfort than I would ever dare admit.

His hand twists and turns the lockets of my hair as the other holds me close.

"I wasn't always like this. I'm sorry you only got to meet this version of me." His voice is soft, possibly softer than I've ever heard it as his words fill the empty void around us.

I don't say a word, worried that anything I do say may trigger his anger.

"I'll go in willingly with them, I won't fight it. Just let me hold you one more time before it's your time to go." His words send a cold shock through my body - startles me in the worst possible way. He can't possibly know. He wouldn't allow it. He can't.

"I know this is goodbye. I'm not going to stop them. I just want you for a little while longer before our time is over," he tells me as he places a kiss on my forehead, bringing me closer once more, leaving no space between our bodies as his breathing evens out while his hands caress my skin.

He knows. He knows, and he's letting me go.

Five

CHARLIE

Gray is pacing. Tapping his fingers against his outer thigh and pacing as if the action will gain us our freedom or calm his erratic thoughts. If only.

We had a plan. Well, Gray had a plan that was supposed to be our escape. I waited and waited and when the sun came up, I realised that something had gone terribly wrong. So here we are with plan B. Presumably. This is what he was doing the last time he had a plan. Pacing and panicking.

"What is it?" I ask aloud, unable to cope with the built-up tension he's brought into the room from the moment he entered.

I don't think he has even heard me. He doesn't make a single notion that signifies he did. He's still pacing. Back and forth, from one end of the living area to the other, over and over again.

"Gray," I say gently as I walk over to him, placing myself in his line of sight. I don't want to startle him.

Despite how much he's attempted to hide it, it's clear to me that he's been as much of a mess as I have since the moment I woke up. He's had to be here and endure it even longer than I have.

He stops abruptly in front of me, looking at me, into my eyes, as if he's searching for the answers to so many unheard questions.

"I don't know if it'll work. I hope it does, but if it doesn't, it'll get worse," he says before taking a step around me as he continues pacing.

It will get worse? The only thing worse than what I'm currently living through is being out there, and even including Liam's many, many flaws, I know for certain that he would do anything to be sure that I didn't end up out there. But that doesn't mean that he can't hurt me. He knows, as well as everyone else being aware, that to get to me or Gray all you have to do is threaten the other. We're each other's downfalls in this wretched place.

"Do you mean a way out?" I wonder, the hope I meant to keep tucked away now firing through every nerve ending in my body.

I hope like hell that's what he's talking about. What else could it be? I can handle things getting worse so long as we know that we've tried, but then the more I think about it, the more I realise that it's not just me that has to be willing. It's Gray too. Am I willing to put him in danger to attempt an escape? I don't think I am, and that thought terrifies me because that's probably exactly how he feels about me.

Gray continues his obsessive walking, thinking over whatever it is that has him so desperately consumed.

"The less you know, the better, but I managed to contact Dad. He can get us out but they need more people, they'll get butchered otherwise. They'll be here in five days," he pants out as he stills and hovers in place, his fingers tapping his thigh again as his head flits left and right, paranoid of anyone overhearing us.

We can get out. As much as I want to know every detail, I couldn't care less about the nitty gritty of it so long as it means that we can leave. I can go home, and that thought fills me with as much dread as it does excitement. Now that the prospect is genuinely a possibility, the option of going home, the thought of being anywhere but here, makes me realise how much I've undoubtedly changed in such a short space of time.

I know they'll want to know everything, and I know that even if I refuse to tell them that they'll have a pretty good guess going off the sight of me now in comparison to the last time they saw me dressed up ready for what now seems like the most silly night. All of this because I wanted a night out. A night to go out with my friends. I could have stayed at home or at Victor's and none of this would have happened. Or, at least if it had, then I would have had so much more protection around me in an attempt to stop it from occurring.

I hate that I question whether they blame me. I had to convince both Crow and Victor to let me go that night, and look at what happened. Look what happens when I get what I want. I'm completely transformed. I left my father childless and alone all because of my selfish wants and needs. It was bad enough that Gray had already disappeared, but to have both of us gone must have been heartbreaking.

"Do you think they blame me?"

Gray stops, his brows creasing together as he looks at me.

"Blame you for what?" he asks, the confusion evident in his tone.

"For this," I say as I wave my hands around the space we're in. "I'm only here because I wanted a night out." I laugh bitterly.

"Char, no. No, fucking hell, no. I hate to admit it but one way or another, these people, these fucking animals," he snarls, "would have got you. Christ, I've been here for months, and I've never even met the top dog and even the mention of them has me fucking shaking. He's a stubborn fuck by the sounds of it. I can tell you that nothing you did or didn't do would have made a difference. It might not have been that day, or even that week or month, but you would have ended up in their grasp no matter what. But now is our time to get out, Charlie. Now is our time to move on from this. You're with me, right?" I nod feverishly at his words, my head bobbing of its own accord as my chest fills with emotion, with love for my brother that's been as tortured as I have, if nothing else by simply knowing what I've been through while here.

"Midnight. Midnight in five days' time, and they'll be here. Just act normal until then and the rest is sorted, OK? Just be who you need to be to survive until then. Can you do that?" I nod again, not trusting my words to come out with as much strength or conviction as I would like.

"OK, right, now sit down and play a game with me, you know what Liam's like if he thinks we've been scheming," he mutters as he takes to the table and pulls out the board game. I follow him over, taking a seat opposite him, watching and imagining the reunion I've wanted for so long as he puts the board out between us.

He's right. Liam hates when we're just sat chatting when he walks in. He always asks what we're planning, what we've been talking about when in actuality up until today, we've very genuinely just been talking to each other. He's a paranoid man - admittedly with good reason because he knows as well as I do that I would love nothing more than to leave, but I'm certainly not going to be the person to give in to his paranoid state.

Five days and I leave. I hope. The last plan was the furthest thing from successful. Gray had a plan, told me the day and time, a day and time that Liam somehow also knew about and then it came and went. Nothing happened. It turns out the guards had changed rotation which put the whole idea in jeopardy.

This one might work, and then I'll really say goodbye to Liam. And then what happens to him? I hate that any single part of me even wonders, let alone cares. I'm going to need some serious fucking therapy when I get home.

My mind wanders back to the thoughts of Gray and the potential consequences of his plan going wrong. Come to think of it, aside from being aware of him having his own apartment in here, I've never asked what he does, what's taken from him.

"Gray, where do you go when you leave here? What do you do?" I ask.

I watch as his eyes lifts slowly to meet mine.

"I usually go and stay in my apartment. They ask me to do menial jobs - cleaning up, doing the accounts, crap that no one wants to do. I don't have the same problem you do," he tells me.

We haven't spoken about it. He's not asked, and I've not divulged the information, but I have no doubt that he knows and by the look of wrath filling his eyes, I know that he doesn't like it any more than I did to begin with.

"He's not all bad. He's better than what you've told me happens out there. Much better. He does care about me in his own fucked up way. I know how to get around him, how to get what I want sometimes," I tell him honestly.

He nods his head at me, likely unsure of what else he can say or do. We're both stuck here with no one to save us. Yet.

"I know he's not what I thought he was, but that doesn't change the fact that I don't like what I suspect happens when I leave." He rolls the dice, effectively stopping the conversation there as he makes his next move on the board.

Six

CHARLIE

"I'll be out in a second," I call back to Liam through the bathroom door. He doesn't like leaving me in here for too long. He's probably afraid that I'll find a way out or possibly drown myself in the bath. I couldn't pretend that I hadn't at least thought about trying both of the above. I have never been so uncertain of myself, my mind and my mental strength or the lack of it, since being held as a prisoner.

They don't happen often - panic attacks - and when they do, Liam is usually at work so I am alone or Gray has been here once, but I can't cope with this while he is around.

"What are you doing?" Liam questions as he taps on the door again.

The tears brim to the surface and don't leave as I feel my breathing speed up. A sudden and overwhelming sense of anxiety and helplessness overcoming every part of me.

I can't do it. I can't be here. I can't be in this room or this place or in my mind. My mind is shutting down, my body not far behind it.

I can feel my body shaking, and violently so as I quiver in a seated position underneath the spray of the shower. The water is the only thing keeping me from losing it entirely. It's freeing knowing that it comes from the outside world. The only thing from the outside world that is coming for me.

My chest feels like there's a stampede of beasts stomping on top of me, my heart beating so quickly from the never-ending pressure on me that I can hardly breathe. The breaths coming out of me are short and sporadic in nature, leaving me feeling even more panicked than before.

"Open the door or I'm coming in." Liam.

But I can't move. I can't speak or think or do anything aside from ride the wave of the all-consuming panic and pain filling me.

My chest pumps as the sobs shake my body under the water, my eyes closed, unable to distinguish and explain or cope with the situation I'm in.

Breathe. I just need to breathe.

Fucking breathe.

"Charlie." His voice sounds so close but with my eyes closed, I can't figure out if he managed to get in. I locked the door. Did he unlock it? Is he in the bathroom?

Open your eyes.

But I can't. My eyes won't open, unwilling and unwanting to see what's in front of me.

"Charlie. Look at me." His voice sounds panicked, afraid almost as I feel his hands find my shoulders. He shakes me. He's inside.

I force my eyes open, seeing Liam crouched down in the bathtub beneath the shower opposite me fully clothed, now soaking wet too.

"You're having a panic attack. That's what this is, right?" I nod, not trusting my voice as the tears continue to roll down my cheeks, falling into the tub alongside the shower water still spurting out.

"Charlie, I need you to breathe for me. Breathe in, copy me," he instructs as he takes a deep breath and encourages me to do the same.

I try to follow his instructions but all I can feel is the pain and fire in my lungs.

"I can't," I sob, my words coming out practically unintelligible as he shakes his head, lifting his shirt over his head and throwing it aside before reaching over and pulling me onto his lap.

"Feel me. Feel my hands on you, feel my heart beating, Charlie. You can hear my voice and no one else's," he tells me firmly as I fall into his chest, my legs pulled up beneath me.

His hands stroke my hair, my back, my shoulders.

"Touch me, baby girl. Don't think about anything else. Touch me and know that while you're here, while you're in my arms, that I will never let another soul near you," he whispers, his hand pulling mine up to his chest, my palm above his steadily beating heart.

"Match me, baby girl. You used to try and make our hearts and breathing match when you were little. You used to copy my breathing pattern. Do it now. Feel me, trust me, and copy me." I listen to his words, let them consume me as I take nothing else in.

He's right. I remember him cuddling me as a child and trying to make myself breathe at the same time as him. His breaths always seemed too slow, meaning that I'd end up out of breath quickly, but I ignore that and do it again. I imitate his breathing, feel his hands as they slide over my shivering body, and feel his heart beating beneath my hand, his chest rising and falling at the same time as my own.

"I will never let anyone get to you, Charlie. I might be the bad guy, but I know you know I'm being truthful when I say that you can trust me in this moment. I would skin any man or woman alive that dared to even think about harming you." His words are harsh, though what's even more brutal is the truth in them. He's right and despite the way he's treated me, even if just for his pride or his fucked up way of caring for me, I do know that he wouldn't ever let anyone else hurt me.

"Breathe with me, baby girl, keep breathing." I don't say anything as I take his continued commands in and do as he instructs.

The world seems a little clearer, not as hazy or blinding and within minutes that feel like hours my breathing has regulated to match Liam's.

"No one will ever get to you again. The only devil that you need to worry about in your life is me."

"Is that supposed to help?" I strangle out, my voice croaky from the tears.

"You might not realise it but you have limits, and I'd never push you past them. I know what you can handle from me and what you can't. You might feel like I've pushed you out of your comfort zones, but I have never and won't ever tip you over the edge."

I think his words over, my mind reeling back to the torture he had inflicted upon me until I had given in. He truly didn't think he had pushed me too far. Had he? Despite these panic attacks that are more based on my lack of control than Liam, I have always known, even in the worst events with him, that I could stop it or at the very least make him stop even if the actions that happen afterwards don't stop. I think.

I knew that he didn't want to hurt me permanently, maybe I did know subconsciously that I could get through it and he did too. Or maybe he's just saying what he thinks will help. I'm not sure any part of me will ever truly know.

His hands comb through my wet hair as he carefully detangles it with his fingers. The slight tugging as he undoes the mess brings my breathing down, using the unusual comfort to help tame my wildly beating heart.

"Come on, you're going to bed. You need to rest," he tells me with a huff as he lifts my body, still clinging to his as he stands and steps outside of the bathtub and begins the walk towards his bedroom.

"Why are you so nice to me sometimes and so willing to

hurt me at others?" I ask, braving the question even though I know it could end badly if it makes his temper flare.

He doesn't stop, doesn't answer me either. He places me on top of the duvet on his bed, pulling the covers from the other side to wrap me up so I'm practically cocooned in the embrace of the warm and familiar material.

I watch as he walks away and returns only moments later with a glass of water and what looks to be two paracetamols.

He sighs, eyeing me with a curious smile before sitting beside me. The bed dips with his presence and weight and for the first time in a long time, not a single part of me feels afraid with him so near.

His jaw tics and tightens as his eyes roam over my face.

"What started this? What are you worrying about?" he asks, the question catching me off guard as I look up at him with my brows creased.

"Are you joking?"

"Obviously not, Charlie," he tells me sternly, his hand circling in front of him as if encouraging me to speak.

"Liam, I've been kidnapped, taken away from my family, raped, beaten and forced into sex with no idea of how or even if I'll get home." My voice is surprisingly strong and loud. I almost expected to break down saying all of that out loud, but Liam's face doesn't alter, his face a mask as I watch his Adams apple bolt up and down as he takes in my words.

"You miss them. Crow and Victor. Your dad and that Alice girl. Is that what this is?"

My bravery seems to have no bounds as my eyes roll of their own accord.

"Of course, that's part of it, but it's not just missing them, Liam. I don't want to be here. I don't want to be made or coerced into doing things I don't want to do. I don't want to feel like I'm cheating on anyone. I don't want to have to avoid thinking about them because the moment I do, I feel so guilty and dirty and filled with shame." My eyes become glassy as I continue, determined to be honest with him since I imagine it's the only chance he'll give me to do so.

"I feel like I'm in a never-ending cycle of torture and pleasure and even the pleasure I hate because I know it's just my body reacting and not what I really want. I hate that I find comfort in you even though you're so awful to me. I hate that I'm not reacting to this the way I should. I should be crying every day and trying to find a way out and yet I just act like your 1960s housewife, making you food and cleaning up and waiting for you to demand sex or a blow job and more than any of it, I hate the times when I don't hate it at all because no matter what you do or say to me, there will always be a part of me that treasures and cares for you. I despise the fact that I enjoy you pleasuring me. I hate that I have no idea what I'm thinking from one minute to the next. I don't even know how I feel about being raped because I've not had time to acknowledge it because I feel like I'm constantly in danger. I feel like if I hadn't gone to that stupid party that I wouldn't be here. I want to go home, and yet I dread it too, because I know that I'm going to have to face my dad and Victor and Crow, and I have no idea how I'm going to feel or what I'm going to say because I can't even understand how I feel or what I think, let alone have any idea how to explain it to them." I take a deep breath, feeling as though I hardly let my lungs inhale a good dose of oxygen as I spoke.

I watch Liam process my thoughts as his eyes scan my face, as if in search of something more.

I feel surprisingly better for letting it out. Gray and I have spoken briefly about everything going on but with the fear of being caught talking about something someone doesn't like, we hardly ever get to truly talk about how we're feeling or what we're thinking. I've just admitted more to Liam than I've even admitted to myself since being here.

Liam runs his hand through his hair as he sighs, his hand rubbing against the back of his neck as he looks down, seemingly speechless as I watch and wait patiently. He must have something to say.

"I can't make this better for you, not how I want to. You know that if I don't have you, they will and I won't allow that. But what I can tell you is that none of this is your fault and when you go home, because you will go home, you don't have to tell anyone anything or explain anything to anyone if you don't want to. If they can't accept you while you heal then they don't deserve you at all." His words surprise me. He says them with so much brash honesty and conviction that it very genuinely shocks me.

His hands reach out, hesitating before touching me. He reaches for my jaw, stroking his thumb against my skin as his eyes dart between my eyes and my lips.

"Get to sleep. I'll read," he says, though I'm certain he wants to say more, his face filled with concern and something else that I can't quite place before he stands from his place, tucks me into the covers again, and leaves the room without turning back.

Seven

CHARLIE

Cottage pie. It's been one of my favourite meals since I was a child and as I portion the meal onto two plates for myself and Liam, I let the familiar smell take me back to a time when Liam and Dad used to argue about who made it best, when there was nothing more complicated or dreadful in my life than my mother not being a part of it. Gray always voted that Dad made it best. I always took Liam's side. Even though his tasted like roadkill.

I take the plates into the living room, placing them on the table where I've already put the cutlery and our drinks, knowing Liam will be back at any moment. He always returns by 7pm. It feels so wrong to be so easily domesticated for a monster and yet the more time I spend with him, the more he opens up to me and shows me kindness, the more I wonder if maybe I've seen everything that's happened in a light filled with negativity for reasons that aren't all that logical. At every turn, he's tried to protect me, even if his ways haven't been the best.

He's been violent, something I've hated at times and yet craved at others. His domineering presence and demands don't give me time or the emotional and mental time to think or rather overthink as my mind seems to do, and I hate that I like that. I hate that I need his demanding nature to truly allow my mind to be free while submitting to him. I asked Gray if he thought I was submitting to Stockholm syndrome more than I was submitting to Liam, and he simply told me that Liam and the situation we're in was no more a choice for Liam than it was for us. I wasn't sure what he meant since he refused to explain further, but it made me wonder if perhaps there was more to the whole thing than I had realised.

As I fold two napkins for each of us, the front door bangs open, the handle hitting the wall behind it as Gray enters, holding up an injured Liam at his side.

My eyes protrude from their resting place as I take in the scene in front of me.

There's blood covering Liam. His head, his neck, his chest. I can't tell where it's coming from or how bad the injuries are beyond the darkening and deep red that is seemingly everywhere.

"What the hell happened?" I ask as I rush towards them, taking Liam's other side, his body slumped.

"I'm fine," Liam grunts, his eyes bruising and beginning to discolour as he looks up at me.

"You are the furthest thing from fine, Liam." I tell him as I help Gray bring him towards the sofa.

Liam sits down in a rush, his body pounding down, his blood staining the material beneath him as he puts his head in his hands and his legs spread apart to hold his elbows in place.

I find the first aid kit and ask Gray to get warm water and a flannel from the bathroom as I take out some bandages, not knowing the extent of the damage done to him yet.

"Why did they do this?" I ask, not needing to have it confirmed that it was them. Those in charge of this operation.

Liam says nothing but shakes his head, refusing to answer me as I use the wet flannel to rub away the blood from around his face. The largest of the wounds seems to be a deep cut beneath his eye. I dab at it gently, not wanting to cause him any more pain than what he's already endured.

Gray stands at my side, his menacing silence filing the room.

"Are you going to tell me what happened?" I ask him pointedly as I continue to clean the blood from a stoic still Liam.

"He wouldn't give you up," Gray says, his voice conveying the same mixed emotions he has towards Liam as I do.

And then his words sink in.

"What do you mean he wouldn't give me up?" I ask, the anger that's been building within me brimming to the surface.

There are so many parts of me that hate this man in front of me but I know, without a doubt, that in his own fucked up way he cares for me beyond measure, and whatever happened to cause this, this pain that he's in, just shows the lengths he's willing to go to protect me.

"She doesn't need to know the rest," Liam tells him, his voice sounding as broken and exhausted as I was when I first came into this apartment.

"For once in your life, Liam, give up the pretence and tell me what the hell happened. Please," I ask, needing to understand.

I was under the impression that he was one of the perpetrators in this scenario, but if they're willing and able to hurt him this badly because of me then that surely isn't the case. Maybe Gray wasn't as far off the truth as I thought he was when he suggested that Liam had as little choice in being here as we did.

"It was me or you. Either I gave you up for them to have you or I gave myself up. That's it. Nothing more, nothing less. I just need to go lay down for a bit and then I'll be fine," he tells me as he rises to his feet, his stance unsteady as he does.

"That wasn't fucking it, and you know it," Gray says.

Liam's eyes become deadly as his head rises to find Gray's eyes, the argument passing between them needing no words.

"I said that was it so that was fucking it. Say another word about it and I'll fucking end you here, Gray. I might not be in charge, but I've got more fucking power than you do," he tells him, his eyes lethal and filled with promise.

"I'll get him to the bedroom. Stay here." Gray huffs out as he takes Liam's arm over his shoulder and leads him away from me, cussing and muttering something to him that I'm not close enough to hear.

From behind I see even more damage. His clothes are completely covered in dirt and blood, the jeans he's wearing showing none of the denim blue that was there just this morning.

I take the bowl of water and the unused first aid kit to the kitchen as I run over the situation in my mind. There's not a single part of me that can look at Liam when he's like that, when he so willingly goes through so much torment and pain for me and want anything but better for him. I have no idea how he got here or why, but I do know that he doesn't deserve it.

I realise now that until I'd come here and spent time with Liam and Gray in a hostile environment that I looked at Liam and his wrongdoings as so black and white and yet when I look at him now, I know for a fact that he didn't get here, to this place mentally or physically because of his evil but rather for reasons he won't share with us.

"He's in the shower. I put the chair in there which will probably be ruined in minutes but he wanted to get in there and couldn't exactly stand, so yeah," Gray tells me as he walks out, his eyes casting glances in each direction as he walks towards me as if checking the room for possible danger.

"I'm going to go, but call me off Liam's phone if either of you need me, yeah?"

"Yeah, of course. Thank you for helping me with him. Can you come back tomorrow?" I ask, wondering if Liam will finally allow the pretence he's used for so long down now that we seem to be on the same side or as close to it as anyone can be in such extreme circumstances.

"I don't think Liam has the energy to care if I come by or not anymore. He wants out as badly as we do," he tells me.

I nod and take him into a hug at the door before he leaves, hating that he's alone.

"They did to him what they did to you when we found you. It's not the first time. He's a monster, but he's a monster that is somehow in love with you and willing to go through anything so you don't." He holds my head close in his embrace as he whispers the words to me before looking into my eyes, nodding when I'm sure mine are wide as saucers in realisation of what he's admitting to me.

"They raped him?" I ask, my words barely there as tears spring to my eyes, unable to comprehend the pain he's repeatedly allowed himself to go through to keep me here. Safe.

Gray nods, his eyes dark, angry I realise. I doubt anyone will ever understand it, but I know as well as he does that we both care for Liam far more than either of us would care to admit. It's fucked, like completely and utterly deranged of us to care, but the longer I'm here, the more I see and get to know the Liam that is truly him rather the one I thought I had known my whole life, the more I realise that he's an entirely different man under the armour.

"He spent his childhood being abused in the same way. Dad told me about it years ago and now here... he went through it over and over again before you got here. They kept telling him if he did then they wouldn't take you and when they did, he knew it wouldn't end. Now you're here, they use you as his weakness. They know they can do anything to him because he'll allow it to protect you from the same fate. They've just not gone this far before by beating him too." His words stun me as I take in the reality of what they mean. My stomach drops, feeling empty and hollow yet so sickly at the same time as I think of what he's repeatedly been through, not just throughout his childhood but since being here, for me.

"How have I never noticed?" I ask aloud, unsure if I truly want the answer or not.

"He's used to putting up a front. It's something he's done for years, Char. I don't have a fucking clue who he really is, but I have a feeling it's not someone that's as bad as we think, or at least not someone that's just bad, you know?"

"Yeah, yeah I understand." He gives me another hug, waves goodbye, and walks away as I shut the door and find myself on the floor with my back to it, my knees curled up to my chest as I contemplate the information I've just been given.

I hear a door shut in the apartment and as my head lifts, my eyes connect with Liam's, his body now clean of blood as he stands in the doorway to the living room with nothing but boxers covering him, the bruises and damage from the torture he's endured clear on his skin.

"Don't you fucking dare, Charlie." His voice is ice cold and filled with venom as he stares at me, his words making no sense in my mind.

"I'm not doing anything." It's as I speak the words that I realise I'm crying, the tears causing my voice to crack.

"He told you. I fucking told him not to say anything, the stupid fucking bastard." he mutters as he walks towards me, his steps still a little unsteady but far better than when he walked in.

"Stop looking at me like that. Stop feeling sorry for me, I don't need it and I don't fucking deserve it. Stop it," he orders as he crouches down in front of me with a hiss, the movement obviously causing him pain which only fills me with more sorrow and sadness.

"You don't get to decide what you deserve. If I want to feel sorry for you then I damn well will," I tell him, bravery and anger that I've not felt for a long time brimming and bubbling as I answer him back. Something I wouldn't have dared do mere hours ago. But I realise now, I know with complete certainty that he's been so hard on me because he knows nothing else, because he's been so determined to be sure I don't land upon the same torture that he has at the monsters' hands.

"Why are you so stubborn?" he asks with a small smile as he sits opposite me on the floor with his knees bent in front of him.

"Why are you so secretive?" I answer back with my own question, one I genuinely wish he would give me an answer for.

He huffs out a grunt as he watches me, his head shaking. "Why the hell do you have so much empathy for me?"

I sit silent for a moment, pondering his question.

"Either because I legitimately have Stockholm syndrome or because you're genuinely not as bad as I thought," I tell him honestly, curious about how he'll take my words.

His lips lift up in a boyish grin and then his body shakes as his head falls back, a laugh finding its way out of him.

"You think you have Stockholm syndrome? You've thought this through?" he asks as he wheezes, his laugh filling the air and lifting my sadness along with it as I smile at him.

I remember seeing him smile and laugh before he went to prison, but I'm not sure I've seen it or perhaps just paid attention since he's been out and yet as I watch him laugh now, see the happiness in his face, my stomach fills with unwelcome butterflies as I realise that I wish I could do this constantly. Make him smile. Make him happy.

"I don't know why you're laughing. I mean, I've been kidnapped, it's a legit option here, Liam," I tell him, though seeing how free and open he looks as he laughs at me and my thought process has me denying the possibility.

"No, you're right, it's just funny that you've actually thought this through. I thought I'd broken you, and maybe I have in some way, but I don't think you're as broken as I thought you were. And since when do you answer me back? What's happened the last two days?" he asks, his voice light and happy.

"I'm pretty sure I'm broken beyond repair at this stage, but I still have a mind. I answer you back in my head mainly but I feel like I've seen you, like really seen you and you can't go back to being a dick now," I tell him honestly.

His smile drops as he watches me. He nods his head before letting it fall back again, his eyes looking heavenward before finding me again.

"I really didn't want to hurt you." He stops himself then, a small grin overtaking his face, transforming him completely, showing me how handsome he truly is when he's joyful and carefree. "OK, that's a lie. I'm a sadist in the sack but I mean, I didn't want to hurt you like I have. I didn't want to hurt you permanently, just for pleasure. I just didn't know how else to make you give in," he tells me, his honesty shocking me.

"A sadist in the sack," I repeat. He looks at me with a sly grin as he gets up, grabs my hands and lifts me to my feet, bringing us chest to chest. Or rather, bringing my head to his chest as I look up at his much taller frame.

"That's right. I don't know if you noticed, but I did say other words too. I like how it's just those words that you pick up on though," he tells me as he puts his hands in my hair and plays with the strands he finds.

"I'm well aware you said other words, I just got stuck on those. Does this all mean you'll stop being a dick and work with me now?" I ask.

His eyes lift above my head, searching the empty space beyond us as his teeth catch his bottom lip.

"Can I hug you now?" he asks, his eyes penetrating my own, this being the first time I recall him asking if he can touch me in any way. I take his question as an answer. It's the first time since I've been here that he's given me a choice rather than taking, manipulating, or forcing my touch.

I give him my answer without words as my arms reach around his back, meeting behind him as my face falls to his warm chest, his skin warm to the touch. He sighs into my hair before placing his arms around me, his body quivering and his breath catching as I land a small kiss on his chest.

"I'm feeling like I need to be a bit more frank with you considering we've just had a breakthrough, so ask me anything. Whatever you want, and I'll be honest. I'll tell you whatever you want to know. I can't be fucked with this anymore. Anything."

My mind whirls with possible questions, knowing that I have more than we could possibly have the time to ask.

"Is Crow really an O'Banian?" I ask, remembering the phone call with him from before I was taken.

Liam pushes me away, looks into my eyes, and nods at me with hesitance.

"Yeah, he's the son. Well, one of the sons." He nods.

Even with the hatred running through my veins for him before any of this happened, I believed him and I still do.

"How did this happen? Any of this?"

His hand reaches for my neck. He slides his fingers to my nape, running them along the back of my neck and my lower scalp before he speaks.

"Come and sit down. It's not exactly a short story."

Eight

CHARLIE

Liam passes me a mug full of hot chocolate before taking a seat beside me on the sofa. I turn my body so that I'm facing him, my stomach filling with dread as I wait for the answer I've wanted to know for what feels like an eternity.

"I'm going to start right at the beginning. If you need me to stop or explain anything then you can ask, but it might take a while. It's... complicated," he finishes with a jerk of his head as he finds the word most suited to the story I'm patiently waiting to be told.

"I was abused as a kid. Gray probably told you that, but he nor your dad knew the extent of it. It wasn't just beatings and rape. I was groomed from the first moment I can remember to be what my father and his men wanted me to be. He was powerful. A business man that had more money than sense. More fucking insanity and hatred and want for more money than he ever really needed. So he used me. His friends had the most fucked up fantasies - all involving children. Me. So he charged them. They'd get time with me to do whatever they wanted, and he'd get a hefty cheque at the end of it. I never went to school. He hired a tutor and for the longest time, I would cry myself to sleep wondering how other kids coped with this, because I assumed it was normal. I didn't know any different."

He takes a breath, watching my reaction or purposeful lack of a reaction on my behalf. The sorrow I felt filling me made me want to cry for him, but I knew he wouldn't appreciate that and probably wouldn't continue if he saw me react that way, so I schooled my expressions.

Dad had hinted at Liam having had a bad upbringing, but I thought he meant divorced parents or an alcoholic father or a dead parent. Not for one moment did I assume it was ever this bad. I want nothing more than to comfort him, but I also don't want him to stop talking. He looks as though he needs to get it out as much as I want to hear it. I need to know what makes him tick, what makes him him, and what brought me to the situation I'm in now. I know that if I attempt to comfort him, he will take it as a sign of me not being able to cope, or he'll hate the sympathy and stop telling me anything, which is not what I want.

"So, this went on for years, until I met your dad. My father had asked me to go out and run some errands. I'd already tried to run away and was left nearly dead for it so I didn't ever try again. Your dad was there. We hit it off immediately, even though I had no fucking clue how to act around anyone aside from my dad, his friends, and the very few people I'd met outside of that circle of people. Your dad lived right by the depot my dad sent me to to do errands and every time he saw me, he'd come out, take me inside, and feed me more food than I knew what to do with. I went there one day after a particularly bad beating. I was used the night before more brutally than I'd ever been and the moment your dad saw me, he told me he'd get me away from there. And he did. I never saw my dad or his men after that. I lived my life with you and your dad. Your mum, too, until she left and I thought I was healing. Until I was walking home with you from the shop one day and saw my dad stood right outside your front door. I shoved you inside of one of the men's houses closest to yours, told them to protect you with their life, and walked up to my father as if I wasn't more terrified than I ever had been in my life."

He takes a moment, his brows creasing together as his eyes look skyward, his gaze completely dazed as if recalling the events of that day as they happened exactly, unwilling to miss any small detail out now that he's started.

"What did he want?" I ask, though I have a creeping feeling that I know.

He looks at me after I speak, his eyes withdrawn somehow even though his gaze feels intense.

"He wanted me to work for him. In prison. If I refused, he would take you. He'd obviously been watching me for long enough to know that no matter who I was close with - your dad, Gray, the men at the club.. he knew you were my one true weakness. He insisted that he had men that could get you with a moment's notice, that he'd let me go when I had done what he wanted and that if I didn't do what was needed then he'd make sure his reach got you too and I had no doubt it would." His words shatter me completely. He'd lied - sort of at least when he'd told me the reasoning for his jail sentence when he first got out. But now that he is here, as his story is unfolding, I am beginning to understand and my heart breaks at the thought that I'd ever questioned him.

He had sacrificed himself for me in more ways than I ever truly realised, and I'd done nothing but question him and be unwilling to believe or understand his side of the story. I remember my dad telling me as a child that there were always two sides to every story and I realised now that I had never given him the chance to truly, openly give me his.

"That's why you were going to take me? So Gray and Crow were right, they just didn't understand why they were right." Liam nods as I put the pieces together - pieces that in all fairness, no one could have guessed or assumed without the knowledge that Liam is giving me.

"I planned on taking you away, but I got caught by two of my dad's men and they tried to take you instead. I killed them both and didn't fight or run when I was arrested. I worked for my father inside of prison and did everything I could to creep you out and push you away when I came out despite how much I wanted to do the opposite so that when he saw my life, he didn't see you actively in it. He knew I'd be living with you and your dad, but I needed you to despise me. I needed you to hate me or think badly of me. I didn't want him to know that you mattered, but he'd set a price on your head before I even got out of prison."

"A price on my head?" I question, reminding myself of how I ended up here or at least why I suspected I did. The money. The black market. The various people after me because of the price on my head. I had assumed it was something to do with the club, a rival or competitor, but it had nothing to do with me all along.

"We're in my father's domain, baby girl. That's the reason I can't get out."

I take in what he's said, trying to process why I'm where I am, and realise that it's because of his father wanting to hurt him. It's not my fault. Hell, it's not really got anything to do with me. I had assumed that it was a personal attack on my dad or the club, but I couldn't be more wrong.

It's not my fault.

It's not his either, but this time when I tell myself that it isn't my fault, I believe it. It was some fucked up attempt at Liam's father wanting to get to him. I could have been anyone Liam cared about, and although I can see why Liam has that grimace on his face as he sits there and undoubtedly blames himself, I know that it isn't his fault either and that he's protected me from the worst - giving me the lesser of two evils. Always. He has been taking my place to ensure that I'm kept safe or as safe as he can keep me.

My heart soars as I watch him, his face in his hands with his elbows on his knees. He looks completely shattered. Broken. Beyond repair, and so much of me wants to fix that.

"Why didn't you tell my dad? How did Gray end up here?" I ask, realising that there must be more he needs to tell me.

Liam doesn't move from his crouched over position but does begin to speak.

"When I saw my father all those years ago and even up until you got here, he insisted that if I told anyone, if I did anything to jeopardise him, he would make sure you all went through a worse fate than death. I had no idea who I could trust. He made me a paranoid mess, thinking that everyone was out to get me. I had no idea what to do. I know I could have done things better but in the moment, I had no idea how. This isn't some excuse; I know I've done things to you that are unforgivable. I know that, but I'd prefer to be the one to hurt you than them. I can't bear the thought of any of them having their hands on you. I'd prefer to be the villain in your story than them." His voice is barely above a whisper, his admission halting my thoughts.

He has been the villain in my story for so long and I've let him be. He's let himself be. When I spoke to him on the phone, he didn't try to redeem himself or make excuses, he let me think the worst.

"What about Gray? He said he was looking for our mum."

He sits up now, running his hand through his hair before looking at me and letting out a low, humourless chuckle.

"He did. He found her. She's with my dad. I have no idea if it was a coincidence or if my dad planned it that way, but he found her with my dad. They're together," he says with a wince.

My brain seems to be having a momentary lapse in sanity. A manic and crazed laugh leaves my lips as I watch Liam for any signs of a lie, but there are none. He's deadly serious.

"You're wrong."

Liam watches me carefully, obviously realising how utterly confused I am as I attempt (and fail) to process what he's told me. She can't be here. In the very same building that I am.

"Why hasn't Gray told me?"

"He didn't want to hurt you. He didn't want you to know that the person that birthed you, the one that was supposed to love you, was in all of this fucked up shit." He sighs.

"She knows about everything?" I ask.

I knew that she must have been heartless to leave two children behind, but to help or even just know about her two said children being taken, held against their will and her daughter being raped and doing nothing about it is a whole new level of bad. I've not had a child. I'm not a mother but surely, surely that can't be right. I know it's not.

"Everything," Liam says with a small nod of his head.

My eyes flit back and forth, unable to still themselves as I think over the situation I've found myself in.

I need comfort and at this moment, Liam is the one I want that comfort from. I shift across the sofa and plant myself on his lap. He seems momentarily stunned before he wraps his arms around me and buries his head in my hair.

"I know it's not the fairytale kind of love that you probably wish for but I do love you, Charlie. I'll never let anyone harm you ever again, I hope you know that." His promise and truth mean more to me now than anything ever has before - mainly because I believe him. Without saying a word, I curl up on his lap and snuggle up to his chest, listening to his heart beat for me.

Nine

CHARLIE

Assuming everything went to plan, we would be leaving tonight. I am going home. I did everything I could not to get my hopes up too high. It didn't go to plan last time, and there is nothing to say that it will now.

I wasn't sure if Gray had told Liam about the plan to leave. I hadn't, but I hope that he knows. I want him to come with us - to leave this hell hole and live a life away from the father that had controlled his every waking moment. I know he is on my side but that doesn't strictly mean that he is OK with me leaving, so I have stayed silent.

"I'm going to fucking kill them all one day," Liam roars as he slams the door open and walks into the apartment.

His hoodie is, as usual, stained with blood - whose I don't know. His body is recovering, and I can't see any obvious or new wounds on him, so I assume it's not his blood.

"What happened?" I ask as I pause the television to give him my full attention.

"They get off on beating the initiates. They killed one tonight," he tells me, his arms flailing around, signalling towards the door.

My heart sinks at the idea of someone being killed. Even if

they weren't a good person by societies standards, that doesn't mean they deserve death. If the initiates here are anything like the ones that often join the Cobras, they're likely younger people trying to get away from a life they dread going home to.

I highly doubt it's the first time it's happened, but it is the first time he's come back and told me anything about his day. It seems our breakthrough really did mean honesty from here on out.

"Is there no way you can leave? Get out of this and get away from it all? If me and Gray found a way out, would you leave with us?"

"It's not as simple as that. If I left, he'd only find me again." He sighs as he takes a seat at the dining room table, his hands clasped together in front of him on the table as his eyes drift off in thought.

Unsure of how best to alleviate his stress, I do the one thing that I know I shamefully crave and he always wants. Touch.

I stand behind him and let my hands travel over his neck, his shoulders, and to his front. My hands wander over his chest as I press light kisses along his neck, feeling his muscles tense before relaxing under my touch.

"What are you doing?" he asks, his voice strained and thick with desire.

"I'm giving myself to you," I whisper into his ear.

"Willingly." I'm not sure if he's asking or stating a fact as he says the word, so I show him.

I move his hands from the table to his sides and straddle his lap, my hands on the back of his neck.

His eyes are dark - hungry as he looks into my eyes, as if looking for any sign of hesitation on my behalf. There is none. Some deep part of me feels endlessly guilty, as if I'm cheating on Victor and Crow, consensually giving myself to Liam without force, coercion, or physical violence forcing my hand, but the part of me that's at the forefront of my mind now wants him.

I want him.

I want to please him. I want to give him the part of me that he's not yet willingly had. I need to be his as much as I need to breathe.

I can feel his hardening length beneath me, his breaths harsh and uncertain as he watches my every move.

I run my hands through his thick hair as I trace my lips along his jaw and his neck, sucking on the delicate skin ever so slightly. My lips find his. He doesn't move or engage for a moment - and then the world ends and begins with us as he ravages my mouth, his tongue finding mine in a fiery battle of wills for dominance. His hands cling to my hips, the pain from his rough grasp on me setting my core alight above the hard length of his cock jutting towards me, jolting me skyward. His mouth doesn't leave mine, though he does end the hungry kiss, our breaths mingling and violent as he fists a hand in my hair and pulls my head from his.

His eyes sear into mine, his gaze alluring and confounding.

"If you don't really want this, you have to tell me now because once I start, I'm not going to stop, Charlie. You can tell me no a million times, but it's not going to happen unless you say no right now." His words are somehow the sweetest he's ever said, which has got to make me the most fucked up person to think so but for the first time since I got here, he's letting me out. He's letting me say no. He's giving me a choice even if he's not giving me one after that word comes out of my mouth.

"I want you, Liam. I want you inside of me," I tell him shyly, my adrenaline-filled bravery from only moments ago having evaporated and leaving me meek and small once more.

He lets out a sound not dissimilar to a roar as he picks me up, his lips finding mine again as he devours me while carrying me towards what I have to assume is the bedroom.

My body is thrown down onto the bed, the whole bed shaking under the weight of me being thrown its way. I lay there startled but brimming with excitement as I watch Liam undress in front of me, his thick and powerful muscles rippling as he moves and throws his clothes to the ground beneath him.

When he's done and stands stark naked in front of me, my eyes automatically draw down to the erect cock wishing for attention.

"Strip for me, baby girl."

I stand and strip slowly, accentuating every movement I make in the hopes of turning him on even more. When I finally see his face, I realise that it worked. His eyes look practically soullessly dark as he appreciates the sight of me, his eyes appraising every bare part of me.

"You're so fucking beautiful." His words and the low hum of his voice have the desired effect, shooting straight to my core.

"Lay on the bed for me." His command is simple, and yet my mind wanders and jumps as I do as he says.

"Spread your legs for me."

I do just that, waiting with eager anticipation as I bare myself to him. He takes a moment to look, his eyes filled with adoration and lust as he does before his face fills the gap between my legs, his tongue gliding from my clit and back down, the feverish actions of a starved man.

His teeth nip at my bud, my hands grasping his hair as he squeezes the skin on my inner thighs while working me closer and closer to the brink with his tongue and his fingers beginning to fill me.

A sound unlike any I've made before leaves my lips, my desperation leading my hands to claw and pull at his hair, pulling him closer to me as if he could possibly be any nearer.

When my orgasm rears to life, I hear myself as if unpretentious calling his name, my thighs closing in around his head as he rides and laps up the wave of the lust-filled sin that escapes my body.

He rises from his position, holding my legs apart as he settles between them, his cock sliding along my entrance with ease, my wet embrace urging him on as he looks at me with love filling his eyes before entering me in one swift and harsh motion. A low gasp escapes me at the shock of his abrupt entry. He waits a moment for me to adjust before he begins pounding into me, my legs clinging around his waist as I thrust my hips up to match his quickening pace.

His hands take hold of my waist and hips as he rocks our bodies together as one, the actions along with the friction from his body on mine causing a yielding heat to pool between my legs. The slapping sound of his body beating against mine does nothing but make the frenzied look in his eyes more hungry and desperate as he roars to life and flippantly rolls into me repeatedly.

The orgasm within me begs for release, my body pathetically desperate for more as he utters curses, his hand in my hair as he ruggedly releases his load within me, his cock twitching and sending me just far enough for my own orgasm to follow his.

His body falls limply on top of my own, the warmth and security of his body on mine bringing me peace as I close my eyes and smile while he plants light kisses along my face. My eyelids, my cheeks, my lips, my jaw, and my neck.

"Come here," Liam grunts out as he flips us over so that he's on his back and I'm lying on top of him while he's still nestled inside of me.

"I need to go to the bathroom and clean up," I insist with a smile, watching as he shakes his head and looks at me with mocking disapproval.

"No, you don't. You're staying here. I'm staying inside of you and not a single bit of my cum is leaving your body. You're mine, baby girl, and anyone that tries to tear you away from my body right now will be fucking sliced and fed to the pigs."

I can't help the sudden laugh that leaves my lips as he speaks, the seriousness of his crinkled brows and the wonder in his eyes as he watches me laugh.

"Why are you laughing at me? I'm being fucking serious," he

says. "Unless you need to piss, then you can go. I'm not into piss play. But if you go to pee then I'm filling you back up when you come back," he tells me sternly.

"I'm laughing because you sound crazy and I don't hate it," I tell him honestly. He opens one eye to look at me again, his arms wrapping around my body before sighing and closing his eyes again.

"Wait, do you need to pee?" I shake my head with a blinding smile and fall asleep nestled into his chest with his arms cocooned around me.

Ten

CHARLIE

The soft shaking of my body jolts me awake. I had tried to make sure I didn't fall asleep but my eyes closed and surrendered to sleep before I knew what was happening.

My body moves, suddenly aware of what's happening anytime now. What time is it?

"You need to get dressed. They'll be here soon." Liam.

I'm stunned into silence as I listen to his words, confirming his knowledge of us going and yet he's doing nothing to stop it. Why? Why is he letting me go? Is he coming with us? Despite the many terrible things he's done, I can't bear the idea of leaving him here. Or leaving him at all. After the truth and heartbreak of his life, I realise that no matter what he's done, I want him, his life entwined with my own somehow.

He gets out of bed and begins dressing himself in his usual clothes and then pulling out his riding leathers. Why is he putting his leathers on? My mind is racing with possibilities as I sit, stunned, unable to move as I attempt to process what's happening in front of me. I shift my eyes to the clock. 11.45p.m. Fifteen minutes.

"Baby girl, listen to me. As much as I'd love to stay here

with you all night, they'll be here any minute and even though I have no doubt you'll tell them everything, them walking in on you naked in my bed isn't high on my priority list, and I somehow doubt it's what you want either. You need to get dressed," he tells me hurriedly, his hands on either side of my face as his eyes beat into mine before he begins rummaging through his drawers and pulls out some of my clothes.

I take action and get dressed as quickly as I can, part of me questioning if this is some kind of trap, but I'm so uncertain that I have very little idea what to say. No. He wants out as much as I do. Where's Gray?

"Put these on," he says as he hands his leathers to me. So, they're not for him.

"Why?" My voice is more timid than it's been in months, the confusion I'm feeling coming front and centre.

"They're not much but they'll protect you more than your clothes will if shots are fired," he says as he pulls the jacket around me and zips up the front.

"Why are you letting this happen?" I ask, realising too late that it sounds like I'm sad at the prospect of leaving when in reality all I should be feeling is joyous at the idea, yet his apprehension and willingness to let me go confounds me.

Liam stops, turns, looking at me with nothing but sincerity as he steps closer. The heat from his body is felt all over mine even though he's not touching me.

He sighs, his eyes low before he looks into my eyes again.

"I've already taken up too much of your time and inflicted more hurt on you than I wanted to. It's time for you to go home, baby girl. It's time for you to heal and live your life." My mind is blank as I take in his words, unsure of why or how he's come to this conclusion, but thankful all the same.

"Thank you." My words are a whisper, barely spoken, but I know he heard me, his eyes filling with sorrow as he wraps his arms around me and pulls me into his chest. I hug him, my arms around him as I nestle my head into him further, holding back the unshed tears that threaten to spill over.

It's not a moment later that I hear what can only be described as pure chaos in the building surrounding us as the front door to the apartment bursts open.

Gray rounds the corner, a gun in his hand, his eyes scanning the scene in front of him with confusion and a sad understanding - myself pulling away from Liam's embrace.

"Charlie! Is she in here? Charlie!" a voice I would recognise anywhere shouts from the lounge and before I know what I'm doing, my legs are leading the way to him. The moment he comes into view, the tears I previously held captive lose the battle, the tears and emotion pouring out of me at the sight of him as he takes me into a bear crushing hug, the tears that I attempted to hold in falling freely down my dad's shoulder as he hangs onto me for dear life.

"Oh, Charlie," he whispers, his voice sounding hoarse in my ear as he holds my head in place at his nape.

His hands move from my back, placing me down as his eyes turn to black slits of anger when he looks up to see Liam mere feet away from him.

Liam looks at me and nods his head with a weak smile before laying his eyes back upon my father's, his guard down, his eyes forgiving of what he knows will come. And it's him giving up that stops me because no matter who he is or what he's done, the stupid, stupid part of me that could feel empathy for anyone doesn't want this.

"He stopped them from hurting me," I practically yell as my dad's hand halts mid-air with the gun faced directly at Liam's head. I don't dare look at Liam or Gray, knowing that they'll both be as surprised as I am, understanding more of the why than my dad ever will.

My dad's eyes find mine, his arm not moving.

"What happened?" he asks, his words coming out harsher than I've probably ever heard.

"I have no idea, I just know that he protected me and took more beatings to protect me than I ever had to take," I tell him honestly. "And he knows things, it might not be much but it's more than me and Gray know. He knows a lot more than we could tell you. He can help." I feel like I'm manipulating him. My words aren't a lie, not in the slightest but I, as well as Liam and Gray, know that I'm stalling. I'm stalling the end of Liam's life. For some unknown reason that even I can't fathom. Except I do know, my clambering and shattering heart knows damn well why I can't and won't let him die.

"Did he do that to you?" he asks, not moving, though I know exactly what he means. The scar - the one that tears across my cheek. It's the first time he's truly seen it, having only seen me run up to him in a flurry moments ago, not giving him the chance to see the physical change in me.

"No. I don't have a single scar on my body from him."

"Fuck." My dad drops his arm and brings the gun to his side at the exact moment that I hear footsteps to my right.

"Is he on our side or theirs?" my dad asks me, his gaze not leaving Liam.

"Ours. I promise you; he's been forced into this as much as Gray and I have been." I watch my dad as he nods his head, his body posture relaxing as he goes up to Liam and takes him into a hug, patting him on the back. Liam looks as stunned as I feel.

"Charlie?" The voice is low, filled with pain and anguish, a quiet wonder as I turn and lay my sights upon one of the two men that have filled my dreams and nightmares since the first moment I found myself trapped in this hellhole.

The room stills, time slowing as I take in the outgrown and messy beard covering his lower face, the black under his eyes, the ruthless muscles soaring from his clothes and the heavy breathing of Crow. My Crow.

He takes a step towards me, his eyes assessing and curious as he looks me over, his gaze roaming over my body, presumably checking me for injuries.

His eyes seem to land on the scar on my face. It's strange, seeing him now mere feet away from me when it's the very thing I've hoped for and dreamt of since I first arrived here.

I feel my chest heaving, my face shaking, my eyes stinging with unshed tears that come to life for what feels like the millionth time tonight as Crow puts his hands on each side of my face, his eyes not leaving mine.

"Come here, princess." Crows voice sends shivers down my spine as I recall the comfort he brings me just being in his presence. He wraps me in his arms and I feel my body sinking, floating, revelling in his strength as he holds onto me for dear life.

God, I've missed him.

"You're never fucking leaving my side again. Not to fucking shit or piss or fucking breathe. Nothing. Never again," Crow tells me as he pulls me into his arms, the warmth of his body surrounding me as he strokes his hand through my hair.

∼

"This really wasn't necessary. I promise I'm fine," I tell my dad as Gray shakes his head at me from behind him.

I knit my brows together, wondering what he's trying to get across to me with his stern expression and the shake of his head.

"Yeah, well, I'm sorry if I want my recently kidnapped daughter checked over," he tells me sarcastically as he grips my hand tighter.

He's not let go of my hand since we left a few hours ago. I was stuck in what I found out was a hotel Liam's dad owns and uses as their base as we left. I hadn't been allowed to leave Liam's apartment so aside from seeing trees and parked cars outside of the windows, I had no idea where I'd been. Crow and my dad's best friend, Tin, escorted Liam back to the Clubhouse while Dad drove me and Gray to the private hospital The Cobras and a few other MCs uses. It is paid for solely through the cash of multiple Clubs, meaning that only they have access.

I wonder for the first time where Victor is. Considering the way we left things, I found myself surprised that he wasn't with them. I know from the way my thoughts have ventured that I need to talk to him, to be as honest as I could be. I'm not sure that I care for him in the way I do for Crow.

The bright lights in the private room the doctor has taken me to makes my head ache. I am exhausted. I need sleep.

The doctor has examined me, taken bloods, checked all of the freshest injuries to my body, and is due to come back any moment with results. Although my physical injuries are less than pleasant, I know there is nothing permanently wrong with me. I hope. The only shameful thing I am concerned about is contracting an STD. I have no idea where Liam or the others have been and dread the idea that I have been given something potentially permanent that could alter the rest of my life but with my dad and Gray by my side, my mind was thinking positively, even with the niggle of negativity being thrown in every few minutes. I push it back and force my concentration on my dad.

"We're going to have to talk to you properly when we're back. We need to know everything that's happened. Everything you've seen and everything that's happened to you," my dad tells me gently. He must have an idea of what's gone on, even if he doesn't want to admit it to himself.

I keep forgetting about the scar across my face, having lived with it for long enough and having seen it so many times in the mirror as I stare back at myself, but I forget that he isn't used to it. Every time he looks at me, his eyebrows draw together, his cheeks pinch, and his mouth twitches. I can tell he's doing his best not to stare, but I also know how I used to be if I saw someone with a scar. I think back to the way I used to look at Edgar - one of the rival mc president's sons. Admittedly he had a bad enough reputation to want to keep me away anyway but with the reputation he held alongside the burns covering so much of him, it scared me and I often found myself staring in wonder without even realising it. Only Gray and Liam had seen me since the first night aside from the doctor that was there so I hadn't had to witness the stares, but I have no doubt I will now that it is time for me to go home.

Thinking about Edgar gives me the reminder of Alice who I have avoided thinking about at all costs. I still don't know if the Clubhouse had been attacked the night I was taken or if it was just me that had been attacked. If it was the club, I have no idea if Alice is alive or not and, until now, I hadn't had anyone to ask that would know or give me the answer.

"The night I was taken, what happened?" I ask my dad as I rub my fingers along his hands, my attempt at comforting him as I ask him to think back on what must have been a horrendous night for him.

I had spent so long thinking about it in the earlier days of being away from my life that although it stung to think about the events that took place that night, it doesn't hurt now the same way it once did.

"Crow was ambushed. That's how they got to you. A fight broke out in the rest of the club, but only five men were found. They were killed on sight. No one was lethally harmed from our side if that's what you're wondering." He always has a knack for knowing where my thoughts are, and at this moment I am grateful for that.

"Is Alice OK? Is she still with the Cobras?"

My dad looks at me in question as if it's such a stupid thing to ask then shakes his head, wiping whatever thought it is entering his mind away.

"You could say that. There's been.. a truce of sorts since she and Edgar got closer. She hasn't seen him in months though. She said she couldn't bear to since you were gone and she had no idea if he was a part of it or not. He helped us get to you though. All of his men did," he says begrudgingly. Accepting the help and being thankful for the help offered to you are two very different things, and despite how grateful I am to be more free than I have been for what feels like an eternity, I can understand his hesitation at using the support of others to get here. The Cobras will now owe them, and knowing my father and his love for us, he would have offered anything.

"What was the deal?" I ask, concern filling my voice as I watch him for any giveaways or signs of admission.

"There wasn't one, that's the problem. I didn't even ask. They offered their help willingly with no stipulations, but you know what this is like. They'll ask for something. Eventually." The unknown is worse. That's why he is so on guard. He has no idea when the request for a favour returned will come in, nor does he know what it will be, but as a man of loyalty and worth, he will pay it - whatever the cost.

I watch as my dad pulls his hands away from me and begins twitching with them in his lap. I'm not sure if he's just nervous and anxious, considering how tense this must have been for him, or if it's something more.

"Are you OK?" I ask him. His cheeks puff out as he sighs and takes a deep breath before speaking.

"I need to apologise to you, Charlie."

"What for?" Gray told me that Dad would feel guilty for not getting to us sooner, but I didn't once anticipate him being right. I have no doubt that he did everything he possibly could to find us the moment he knew I was gone, as well as Gray.

"For Victor. The marriage. The deal and the merge of the Clubs. I knew you weren't ready, that you didn't want it, and I made you feel like you didn't have a choice despite knowing that. Having you disappear made me realise how much I've done wrong as a father and I'm sorry. I'm sorry to both of you for not being better than I have been," he finishes as he looks between myself and Gray before looking down to his twiddling hands again.

Gray and I share a look, Gray's full of sadness that I understand.

"Dad, it's fine. This is your life. It's hard for you to separate them and us, we get that, but I'm pretty sure I can talk for both of us when I say that things won't be the same anymore, and I don't think we want them to be. We all need change and that includes you, old man," Gray says as he pats my dad's shoulder and throws a small, hesitant smile my way.

Eleven

CHARLIE

I thought I would be thrilled to be home and though a part of me is, the most prominent part of my brain feels lost being in a bedroom that I know is mine. But it seems nothing like mine anymore.

I purposefully stayed downstairs with Dad and Gray for as long as I could, putting off the inevitable return to a space that was once mine but no longer feels that way. Dad asked if we - Gray and I - wanted to go to bed. It's just past 6am and neither of us have slept since we woke yesterday morning, but my mind is wide awake, no sleepiness in sight as I attempt to adjust my mind to the freedom we now have.

We could go anywhere and yet I don't want to venture anywhere at all. When I stopped on the stairs and wondered where I'd rather be, knowing that I didn't want to be here, nowhere felt like home. Not my childhood home I was now standing in, nor the Clubhouse, or the houses of the Cobras men surrounding us. Not my best friend, Alice's home or Victor's. Nowhere.

I've aged only a few months and yet it feels like I've been gone for decades when I look around the room filled with innocence and evidence of my youth and naivety.

Everything is exactly as it was. My bedsheets have been changed but my diary is still out, the books I was reading are still misplaced on the floor and my makeup is still open on my desk counter.

"Are you OK?" Gray asks.

I spin around to find him searching the room similarly to myself. Remembering the years we spent having sleepovers in here and found joy in the simplest things. Only, it's not just me that left and came back a different person. He did too.

"Are you?" I wonder as I watch his eyes spin around the space surrounding us.

His eyes find mine, no doubt mirroring my own with the sadness and guilt.

"I honestly have no fucking idea, Chars. It's going to take some time for both of us. I don't know where we fit in anymore or where we go from here, but we'll work it out, alright? Together," he says solemnly and with promise as he takes a step towards me and engulfs me in his arms.

"Together," I repeat, knowing that he and only he understands what my mind is doing because his is surely doing just the same.

Gray pulls away as I hear the familiar sound of our dad's heavy footfalls on the stairs. Gray gives me a sad smile, knowing unlike anyone else how I'm feeling.

It's at times like these that I can't even begin to imagine how it must be for those that don't have siblings. It makes me all the more grateful to have Gray by my side throughout life.

"Knock knock, you decent, Charlie?" my dad asks, accompanied by a couple of thumps on the door.

"Yeah, come in." I plaster on a smile as the door swings open and reveals my dad stood there accompanied by Tin. Dad said he was there during the rescue, but I hadn't seen him with all of the chaos.

"Oh, look at you both, my little spy and the troublemaker," Tin says as he pulls me and Gray into his embrace and squeezes me enough that I have to tap his back and let him know to loosen his grip a little.

As someone that's been in my life for as long as I can remember, he's like the unofficial uncle I never really had or knew I needed.

I notice as he pulls away and gazes down at us both that his smile is genuine. He doesn't seem to worry about his every move or word, unlike everyone else I've come across so far since being home - not as though that's very many people in all fairness.

"They might not be comfortable with that, Tin," my dad echoes under his breath in the background. He looks uncomfortable as he watches the three of us, seemingly unsure of how to proceed but obviously wanting to protect us and our sanity, even from Tin.

"It's fine, honestly, Dad. The more people faff to me and make me feel like I've been through something, the more it makes me feel like I have. The closer to normality I can get, the better." I feel uncomfortable saying the words despite them being the truth.

I'm usually open and comfortable with my feelings but having to repeat anything to do with the experiences of the last few months makes my stomach churn.

"Agreed," Gray chimes in as he wraps an arm around Dad's shoulders and knocks his head against the side of Dad's.

"See, it's fine, you old whinge bag. Now go make me a cuppa, will ya?" Tin pushes my dad out the door before giving both Gray and I a wink and a smile as he turns his head and leaves behind Dad.

"It's going to be like this for ages, until we've seen everyone again, isn't it?" Gray asks me as he falls back on my bed and pats the space beside him, signalling for me to join him.

I do just that, enjoying the soft material and familiar comfort of my bed.

"Yep, I have a feeling it is. The more I sit here and wallow in my self pity, the closer I'm going to get to losing my mind. I don't want to be stuck in here. I want to live my life," I tell him quietly as I stare up at the blank ceiling above us.

"What do you want to do?"

"I want to be a writer. I'm going to make it happen. I'm so sick of bad, just bad everything, I'm going to make my life good," I tell him with a determined smile.

I have no idea where I'll start or what I'll do to get where I want to be, but I do know that I want to try. I don't want to hold back or wait for anything anymore. If I want something, I'm going to be a stubborn sod and bloody well make it happen.

"What about you? What do you want to do?" I ask him as I flip onto my stomach and watch him as he bites the inside of his cheek and pinches his brows together.

"I honestly have no idea. I've never known. I just know I want more than this now. I don't know what more is though."

"You'll figure it out, I'll help. We need to move on, make our own lives." Gray nods his head at me, agreeing before closing his eyes.

"I'm just going to rest for a bit and then we can make new lives, OK?" he says, sleeping as he rolls over on the bed and pulls a pillow under his head.

I lay my head down but know that sleep won't be coming for me anytime soon. I can very rarely switch off and fall asleep quickly, no matter how exhausted I am.

I think back to what it is I want to do. I want to write. I have more ideas than I know what to do with, but I have no idea if that's really something I could pursue.

When I think about my life in the years ahead, I can imagine myself with children one day. I can see myself living peacefully in the countryside not far from where we are now and despite how much I've always envisioned a future without the Cobras in it, I can't seem to shake the feeling that they'll always be a part of my life and so much of me is grateful for that. The Cobras have been a family to me for the longest time as I've grown up, adapted to the world, and tried to figure out who I am.

~

Dad squeezed me fresh orange juice that tastes heavenly to go with my breakfast - well, it's mid-afternoon but I've just woken up and Gray is still sleeping and since I haven't eaten since last night, I feel practically starved.

I eat the food from the plate in front of me, devour it more like. I feel as though I have a never ending and never full stomach to contend with right now. Being away from constant danger will likely have that effect on you, though, I imagine. I mean, I ate well before but I feel insatiable today.

Through my breakfast, I notice, but make a point not to be obvious that I've noticed, Dad staring at me. I'm not sure he even realises that he's doing it but every time I glance in his direction, he's watching me. Sometimes with a small smile and other times with a gaze filled with worry and wonder. I can't imagine how awful the last few months must have been for him, but I also don't know how to comfort him. I'm not sure that giving him a hug will help. In all honesty, I don't think anything will help aside from him knowing I'll never leave his side again.

"Who gave you that scar, Charlie?" My body freezes at his words, his question.

I'm not sure I want to answer but I also can't not. If I tell him who gave me it, he'll ask how I got it and even though I've had the all clear from the hospital and they have my full reports and want to start counselling to help me talk through things at which point I'm sure I will be honest, I'm not sure how I can be right now with him - and yet I don't want to lie either.

"One of the men that took me," I tell him, figuring it's the truth and hopefully enough.

"Did they.." He pauses, scratching the side of his face along the scruffy beard that's grown. "Did they hurt you in, you know, in other ways, Charlie?" He grimaces as the words come out, his intention with the question clear.

I find myself hesitant to answer. I don't want to answer - not just because I don't want to have this conversation but because I know it'll break his heart. But I also don't want to start lying to him. My mind whizzes with possible answers that I could give him without lying but without telling the truth and yet they all seem ludicrous or unbelievable, even in my own head.

"Just once. I never saw them again," I tell him, sticking to the truth. I didn't ever see them again and I didn't ask what had happened, where they were, or if they were in the same building that I was living in because I didn't want to know.

His face contorts in agony, his eyes closing as he takes a deep and ragged breath before opening his glassy eyes and looking at me again.

"Liam didn't let me out of his apartment there – he said it was too dangerous. I only saw him, Gray, and the doctor the whole time I was there. No one else was allowed in, and I didn't go out. Even if he had let me, it's not as though I would have wanted to." My dad nods at me, his face clearing as he takes in my words.

"They looked after you?" he asks, his voice sketchy and unsure.

"Yeah, they helped me a lot. I wouldn't have got through it without them." It's the first time I've said it or even thought about it and truly meant it. I hadn't thought about it before, but it is true. If Liam hadn't done what he had for me, I have no idea what would have happened to me or how I would have survived. If I had survived at all.

"Charlie, darlin, I need to talk to you about a few things.." My dad sounds so unsure of himself, and I dread to think what comes next as I wait for him to continue.

In a moment that I thought was about to be either heartfelt and comforting or downright dreadful, the front door springs open, hitting the wall behind it with a thunderous roar as scuffling sounds from behind me. I twist in my chair to look down the hallway only to freeze in place as I take in the scene in front of me.

What the hell is going on?

Crow and Liam are scrapping, if you can even call it that, as they are both attempting to get into the house. My dad must have got up without me realising because between the unintelligible shouting, my dad is trying to split the two up, his own voice shouting and joining in with theirs.

It isn't until Gray comes down the stairs, his hair dishevelled and his eyes still half closed, that I lift myself from the chair and make a move towards the three men currently having a very tightly contained shouting match in the hallway. At least they'd got inside the house now. Most of our neighbours are members of the Cobras, but for the ones that aren't, they would not be happy about this chaos on our very literal doorstep.

Gray's eyes travel from the scene in front of us to me, back again and then land on the ceiling as he sighs, rubs his eyes, and comes down towards me.

"What's happening?" he asks, his voice still hoarse and filled with sleep.

"I have got absolutely no idea," I tell him as I continue watching as my dad pushes Crow and Liam apart, one hand on either of their chests.

"Will one of you please tell me what the fuck is going on here?" My dad's voice reverberates off the walls. His back is to me, but I have no doubt he's glaring at them as his head swivels between the two men.

Silence. Gray stood at my side, obviously just as curious about what and why they woke him as I am.

"Well? Someone. Fucking. Speak." Dad exaggerates and articulates his every word, honing the message home that he's not putting up with this shit right now.

"He hasn't been interviewed yet and when I got to the door,

he just fucking shows up when he's supposed to be at the Club being guarded since we don't have a fucking clue who's side he's on, and now he's staking some fucked up, old man shitty fucking claim on Char," Crow says as he takes a breath and steps away from my dad. And then I replay his words in my head. Oh shit.

"I swear to fucking God, I'm gonna lose my mind," my dad says as he pinches the top of his nose and looks heavenward. "Liam, what the fuck Is going on? Why aren't you at the club?" my dad asks, his head swinging to Liam as he does, his hands flying up in the air in exasperation.

Liam looks at me, his eyes tender and sincere before he looks stone cold as his gaze returns to my dad.

"I am not staying away from Charlie for another second, I don't give a shit what you think or want. They're still fucking out there and until someone annihilates the lot of them, I'm not leaving her side. You can interrogate me with her there, she knows everything anyway." Liam's words practically gut punch me.

I had spent so long since being home just becoming accustomed to being away from that place that I hadn't considered the possibility of being taken again. Without Gray and Liam there, I have no doubt so much worse than what did would happen to me. Things that I wouldn't recover from.

"It's an interview, not an interrogation." My dad sighs as he shakes his head in defeat, letting both Crow and Liam pass.

Crow reaches me first, taking me in his arms and filling me with warmth. It feels unbelievably nice to be in his arms again.

After being with someone nearly 24/7 daily for months to being without them for so long, I probably missed his presence the most.

"You alright, man?" Crow asks Gray as he pulls back from me and gives him a bro hug and pats him on the back.

I watch as Liam stands unmoving in the hallway, my dad

telling him that it's not an interrogation. Liam doesn't seem to be listening or caring for my dad's words though.

It's hard to imagine how close they've been for so many years when I see Liam so detached now. It's as though the front he's always put on has been wiped away and he's been left a very nearly empty shell of the man I remember as a child.

And then for the first time since any of this happened, I think of my dad. Really think of my dad. And Liam. And the fact that I've had sex with Liam. Willingly. Encouraged it even.

Oh fuck.

How on earth I hadn't thought of or considered this before is beyond me. I knew he was my dad's best friend. I knew it shouldn't have happened and yet even through the force, I let it. I allowed it and even wanted and begged for it.

I've not spoke with anyone about how things unfolded with Liam. I have no doubt that the people closest to me at least will ask for more details soon enough and though part of me wants to hide the undeniable connection that Liam and I have, I hate to see him in a place surrounded by people and yet looking so isolated and lonely.

I take a step closer to him, my eyes not leaving his as he gives me a small, lopsided smile, unsure of himself and undoubtedly unsure of how I want this to go. It's one thing to be open and vulnerable and true with him when it's just him and me, but it's a whole other matter when those I care for most are around me. And yet, like Gray said - things aren't going to be the same and I'm determined to live the life I want to, doing whatever it is I want to rather than holding back for the sake of anyone else so I do the one thing that I know we both need and rush into his arms, relief filling me when I feel his head come down onto mine and his arms wrap around my smaller frame.

"Where's the shithead?" Liam asks as he pulls back from the short embrace and looks around.

"Who's shithead, exactly?" my dad asks as his brows bunch together.

"Victor," Gray answers for him. I find myself looking towards him while he speaks and see Crow watching me with a curious gaze, his eyes flitting to Liam occasionally before he nods his head as if in answer to his own question and throwing a mischievous grin my way.

"Victor wants a word with you," Crow tells me, his eyes portraying nothing as he watches me, and yet I watch as the look on his face changes when my dad turns to him and gives him a small shake of his head.

"What's going on?" I ask. It seems they both know something they aren't willing to share with me. Why am I not surprised?

"You'd think after being kidnapped and held hostage for so long, you guys would reflect and realise that I need to know stuff at this stage," I tell them both, understanding that it isn't necessarily Crow that isn't willing to tell me but rather my dad, and Crow is simply going along with my dad's orders.

"I'll go get him. The sooner you know, the sooner you can make your own decision about where to go from here," Crow says, his hooded and wary eyes catching mine as he eyes Liam once more before kissing my forehead and leaving through the front door.

Twelve

CHARLIE

Victor looks nervous. Very, very nervous. His eyes keep shifting around the room towards my dad and Crow, who won't stop glaring at him.

"What happened? Why are you staring at him like you want to murder him?" I ask, hoping it'll lighten the mood and one of them will tell me that they don't actually want to murder him, but they don't speak.

I look towards Victor again, realising now that I don't feel the same way for him as I initially thought I did. I'd realised while away that I didn't feel as strongly for him as I did for Crow and Liam, but seeing him in person only cements that feeling.

"Go on. Tell her then," My dad encourages impatiently, his hands sliding in the air between Victor and I.

"It's my fault you were taken," he says, his hands fidgeting on the table in front of us.

My brows crease, not understanding how it could possibly be his fault.

I look at the men around me. My dad. Crow. Liam. Gray. Victor. They're all sat at the table and it seems myself, Gray, and

Liam are the only ones in the dark here. Their faces are as confused as I expect mine is.

But then I look at Crow and my dad again. They know something.

"How was it your fault?" I am tempted to tell him it wasn't, but I have a feeling I'm missing some rather significant pieces of information here considering how tense and awkward everything currently feels. The air around us is filled with a nervous energy that seems to be emitting from myself and Victor in waves.

"My dad wasn't really interested in a merge with the Cobras, but I had a meeting with an unknown source which wasn't unusual. This person explained that he needed a way to get close to you and he needed my potential connections to do it. I, of course, refused initially. I didn't know you and I had no interest in getting involved in whatever this was, but he threatened my father's life and despite how little we get along, I do love him and couldn't see his life being taken because of me, so I agreed." He winces as he looks up at me before returning his gaze back to his hands. "Except then I really did care for you but I still had this in the back of my mind. Crow didn't want to," he looks around awkwardly, "share you, but I did everything I could to convince him. I needed you both to trust me, so when the source explained that I needed to get you to the club alone that night, I told you I was going but never showed. I didn't ask what their plan for you was, but I knew it had to be bad. I just thought that you'd be safe in the club with Crow," he finishes.

I take a moment of doing nothing but staring at him before I speak.

It was him. It wasn't his fault. I don't for a second feel that it was. I am angry with him, sure, but I know that in his situation, I'd do just about anything I could to protect the people I care about as well.

He wasn't the one that set it all up. He wasn't the one that raped me or held me hostage, but he did trick me. Lied to me. Made me vulnerable.

"Who was the source?" Liam asks, his tone lethal as he eyes Victor.

"I don't know. I never got a name. Just some bloke with a skull tattoo over his face. Creepy as fuck if you ask me," Victor says with a shiver.

"Jonesy," Gray says with a nod from Liam.

I have no idea who this Jonesy bloke is, and I have absolutely no interest in finding out. If he is a part of the reason that happened to me then he can stay as far away from me as humanly possible.

"Right. So, what happened to you?" I ask Crow. "Dad says you were ambushed."

"Yeah, this fucker told me at the very last minute what was going down, so as I was freshly out of the shower, I put my boxers on and ran the fuck to my bike. Basically naked, might I add. Got on, got all of a mile down the road, and got fucking ran off the damn road. Wake up in hospital and here we are," he says with a huff, his eyes never leaving Victor.

"What? That's not right. You gave me vodka at the club," I tell him. I remember it. Clear as day. I remember going in and him giving me a drink of vodka.

Crow's head spins to me so quickly I'm surprised he's not got whiplash.

"What are you talking about? You can check the CCTV, Char, I wasn't there. Not at all that night. Not once."

"Alice saw you. She was at the bar, she saw you," I tell him, not understanding what's happening.

I know he wouldn't lie to me. Not about this. Dad would have said something if Crow was wrong. He would know if this had or hadn't happened, and he doesn't speak up to tell me otherwise, so I have to assume that Crow at least thinks he's telling the truth - but he's not. He can't be because I remember him being there.

"You gave me a cup of vodka and then went to the bathroom and didn't come back. I went looking for you but because I was drunk, I accidently stumbled into the wrong room. That's where they were," I say, not needing to go into any more detail than absolutely needed into what happened after I entered the room.

"Do you really think I'd leave you? I take you to the fucking bathroom with me in your house half the time, baby, let alone in a Club packed full of people," he says, his hands reaching mine over the table and rubbing my palm softly.

He's right. Shit, he's right, but I saw him. It was him.

"Do you have the CCTV?" I ask my dad, who's already got his laptop out without me realising.

"Fuck. Who were you around that day, Charlie? That isn't Crow. I don't know what happened or what you saw but that was not Crow," my dad says, his voice weary and scared as he looks at the screen on the laptop.

He spins the laptop around to me and I watch in horror as I take the drink, the vodka from Matt's hand before he walks away. To the bathroom.

"That's not possible. I'm telling you, I saw Crow," I say as I back away and begin shaking my head.

I don't understand. I thought the vodka was spiked. I mean, it probably was but how was it possible that I saw Crow?

"Hallucinogenics can make you see things. He wouldn't have known that you would have seen Crow but that probably just worked to his advantage. He couldn't have guaranteed you'd see anything in particular, he probably just thought it would help. We didn't find out until afterwards but the plan was for them to come and find you when the fighting broke out, it was just bad luck that you found them first. Fuck, that makes so much more sense. When you told me that Crow left you, I didn't understand it, but he didn't leave you. He didn't even manage to get to you," Gray says as he watches the screen with me, terror filling his eyes, mirroring my own.

"How would they have got it in me before then though?" I wonder as I think through the events of the day.

I'd been to the doctors and then been here all day getting ready. The only people that I had been around were Crow and Victor.

And then I see a wincing Victor and I know.

"You did it?" I ask him, horrified. I understood all of it. I understood why he did what he did. I'd do anything I could to protect the people I cared for, but this was just too much.

"You've got to be fucking kidding me," Crow hisses as he jumps from his chair and rounds to Victor, grabbing the top of his typically immaculate white shirt and holding him mere inches from the floor, the chair he was sat on tipped over beneath him.

"No, wait! I want to hear it!" I yell at him as I get up from my seat and lean across the table towards Crow.

"Oh, you'll fucking hear him scream in a damn minute," Crow says as he unsheathes a gun from the holster beneath his jacket and places the muzzle of the gun at Victor's forehead.

"Crow, no!" I shout as I move towards him, knocking the chair over in the process and moving to grab his arm before he truly lets loose.

"No, Crow. I mean it. Don't you fucking dare," I tell him as he looks at me. He stares back down at Victor for a moment before nodding at me.

"Fine. I won't shoot him," he says with a glint in his eye as his arm rears back before crunching his fist into Victor's face. I watch with my mouth splayed open as Victor's head falls back and hits the hard floor beneath us, his face wincing in pain as he hisses out a string of curses.

"Oh, for fuck's sake, Crow. I love you but you're like an out of control, testosterone filled teenager," I inform him as I move him out of the way and crouch down to a hunched over Victor.

"I love you too, baby," Crow says sweetly as he kneels beside me and places a soft kiss at my temple.

I roll my eyes at that being the only thing he got out of what I said. Of course, that's all he heard.

"Are you alright?" I ask Victor. I nudge Crow away and put my hand out for Victor to take.

I might not be all that keen on his actions right now, but I'm also not a complete animal. Most of the time at least.

"I don't know why you care. I'm sorry, Char. Honest to God, I'm genuinely sorry," he tells me as the men around me mutter and shake their heads.

"I know. Don't stress, it's done now. Nothing can take it back. You've just got to move on," I tell him with a strained smile as he takes my hand and stands from the ground. I'm trying to be a better person, OK?

If nothing else, this whole situation has taught me that I can do whatever the hell I like and right now, forgiving Victor for doing something he felt he had to is what I want to do.

"Do you still wanna know?" he asks as he stands to his full height while rubbing his hands through his hair and over his rumpled clothes.

"Yeah, I do. How did you do it?"

"Well, I didn't. I knew they were going to but I didn't. It was the doctor. Well, not him but his assistant. I don't know how they got to her or knew you were going to be there - I hadn't told them that part but they knew and when they were taking blood, they injected something too," he tells me solemnly.

"But I felt fine all day, right up until I had that drink," I say as I turn to the men behind me for guidance.

"I'm not exactly a drugs expert, but I'm guessing the alcohol didn't help and some take hours to kick in I've heard." I nod at Gray's words. I'm not convinced Victor's right, even if he thinks he is. I surely would have known if I'd been drugged in the morning.

"This better not be you forgiving him and getting back to where we were because I am not doing that," Crow says as he eyes up Victor again, his eyes vicious as he looks him over with a disgusted curl of his lips.

"I forgive him just fine, but I did realise that I don't think I care for him in that way. I would love to have you as a friend though, assuming there's no more lying and setting me up to be kidnapped involved," I tell Victor with a rueful smile.

He winces at my words.

"Too soon?" I ask with a laugh.

"Way too fucking soon, Char," Crow answers behind me.

"Right, is there anything else anyone needs to tell me before we move on?" I ask, my eyes swinging between the men around me. My attempt at being confident seems to be waning when I catch Crow smirking at me.

"Don't even start, we're talking later," I tell him as I roll my eyes at his lack of seriousness in a situation I am attempting to be very serious in.

Gray, Liam, and Dad all shake their heads.

"Well, there is one more thing. More for your dad and Liam to know than anyone else but.." Victor cuts himself off as he backs up when both Liam and Dad begin walking menacingly towards him.

"You realise he's about to tell you whatever this is anyway, you don't need to act all hulk on him," I tell them. I hear Crow snicker in the background before pretending to zip his lips closed when I glare in his direction.

"What is it, boy?" my dad asks him.

"Well, the thing is, my dad wasn't interested in a merge but now he sort of is-"

"I might forgive you, but I am not marrying you if that's where this is going," I rush out, watching as Victor smiles and shakes his head at me.

"No, no, I know. It's honestly probably worse. Since you two stepped down-" I don't let him get anything else out before I put my hand up to stop him.

"What is he talking about stepped down?" I step in between

Victor, my dad, and Liam as I look up at them both with the most incredulous look on my face.

"You know, when I asked 'does anyone have anything else to tell me?' This is what I meant. This is the type of thing you're supposed to tell me. Why the hell have you both stepped down?" I hiss out, my eyes closing and my breath hitching with frustration as I take in the absolute fuck fest (in the worst way) that is the situation I'm currently stuck in.

I genuinely spend more time wondering what the actual fuck is wrong with the male specimens surrounding me than I do thinking about real, logical, normal things these days - which is pretty bloody concerning.

"Char, I'm not exactly in a position to lead right now if you hadn't noticed," Liam tells me with a pointed look.

OK, fair. I'm not telling him so but he has a valid point. I don't even need him to explain. I get it.

"Dad?" I ask, though before he even speaks, I know what's going to come out.

"I was only watching over the Club until Liam got out, it was never supposed to be permanent. I never wanted it to be. I need to move on with my life, with you and Gray," my dad says, the harsh lines and dark circles under his eyes becoming apparent. He may only be in his thirties, but you can see how tired he is - from the mayhem of club life and the consequences of it.

"So, who does that leave in charge?" I wonder aloud.

"By our laws, people fight - both physically and through the votes of our men as to who the new MC President is. It usually goes down the line of succession if everyone is happy with that but Gray doesn't want it, he never has and I'm not going to force that on him," Dad says with a glance in Gray's direction.

Gray has always trained hard. He's a much better fighter than I am, but I'm not sure that he's suited to the role even if he wanted to be.

"That's where the problem kind of lies," Victor interrupts.

"Theo, my dad's right hand man, wants to try and become the Cobras new Pres to merge the clubs."

"Would that be bad?" I ask, though from the ashen look on Victor's face, I assume it indeed would be.

"He's a sadistic fuck that gets off on power and hurting people, so yes, it would be bad," Liam says while scratching the stubble along his jaw.

"And what are the chances of him getting in over anyone else that tries?" I have no idea if anyone has put their name forward, but I imagine the Cobras would want one of their own ruling them.

"None of the Cobras want the responsibility so right now, assuming he has the most support and can gain the most allies, we wouldn't have much choice but to accept him," my dad says.

So it needs to be someone that the Cobras trust, someone that can gain support, and someone that can help form allies. Crow's eyes catch mine as I find a sly smile creeping on my face. I have the best idea.

Thirteen

CHARLIE

"This feels weird," Crow says as we walk together towards the lake and the forest we used to visit regularly.

"I know. It feels like nothing and everything has changed all at once," I agree as I take in the scenery surrounding us.

Spring is now in full swing, a fact that is blatantly obvious when looking at the vibrant and newly growing leaves, trees and flowers beginning to bloom once more.

"I'm surprised Liam let us come out alone. He's a stubborn fucker." Crow sighs as he takes my hand in his.

His calloused hand overwhelms my smaller one. I've always thought of myself as someone that's strong, independent, and a fierce feminist, but I'm realising more and more that the safety of a man I care for, a man's larger presence being near me, and offering me their security sends flutters through me.

He's right. I think the only reason he didn't very genuinely superglue himself to my side was only because Dad insisted that if he didn't at least start the interview process that they wouldn't let him near me. That got him moving. And glaring. There was a lot of glaring involved too. He's good at that.

You know that annoyingly attractive and brooding frown that men do? That one.

Crow's hands are rough and yet they are inviting and comforting too. I peek down to see the way our hands connect.

"Yeah, he's a little protective," I agree.

"Are you scared?" Crow asks me as we pass the street of houses.

"Of what?" I wonder as I look around us and wonder what there is to be scared of.

"Everything."

I think for a moment before responding, trying to think of a way to effectively communicate the way I feel.

"I feel fidgety and paranoid - a little bit wary of touch but overall, no. I mean, it might be a weird realisation to come to but I feel like there's nothing I can do to stop bad things from happening. I could train or carry a gun, or have you or Liam with me twenty-four seven, but if someone really wanted to get to me, I have no doubt that they would eventually. Just like they did before. And even though I'm petrified of that happening again without Gray and Liam to protect me like they did, I don't want to let the fear of that stop me from doing what I want," I tell him honestly as I take a deep breath and attempt to force myself into enjoying the fresh air that I've missed. Being stuck inside for so long drove me crazy or at least it felt that way.

"Are you scared of my touch? You know I won't ever push you, don't you?" he asks as he watches me delicately.

I turn to look up at him as we walk and see the concern written all over his face.

"I know," I tell him with a small smile. There's not a single part of me that questions Crow and his motives.

"Can I ask you something else?" he asks as we near the clearing and the entrance to the woods.

"Yeah, of course." I take my hand from his and run it down my side. His hands are hot. Sweaty even, or is it mine? I can't tell.

"Did anything happen between you and Liam? He looks at you like I imagine I do."

His question stops me immediately, my hands freezing for a moment. I'm not going to lie to him, but I also feel like I've put him through so much already that I don't want to put him through more.

"Yes. We slept together. I care about him," I tell him honestly, worry coating my voice as I shift uncomfortably and walk towards the peak and our den, not wanting to see the horror and disgust on his face. I'm being a coward. I did this and I have to live with the consequences. I turn to him again just as he speaks.

"And you trust him?" he asks, his hand ruffling his already ruffled and short hair.

"Yeah, I trust him just as much as I trust you."

"I hate to tell you, Char, but your judge of character ain't great considering the whole Victor fiasco, so maybe we should take it slow with him. I mean, he's admittedly better looking than Victor so I wouldn't mind seeing him fuck you while you suck my dick but even so, we'll take it slow, yeah?" I nearly drop the travel mug I'm holding, my eyes going wide as I turn to see a sly grin covering his lips.

What did he just say?

I don't know where to start processing his words.

I splutter out some sounds, unsure of what I'm even trying to say as he smirks and wags his eyebrows at me.

"If I'm a bad judge of character, you realise that it includes my judgement of you, right?" I ask with a crooked brow as I fold my arms.

"I'm amazing, thank you very much," he says with a laugh as he takes the mug I'd put on the floor and begins filling it with tea.

"Also an O'banian though," I say. Not a question - a fact. I don't think he'd lie to me at this stage, but I still don't pose my words as a question, not wanting to give him the chance to lie.

I guess this is as good a time as any to bring it up. I watch as his face contorts and he shakes his head with his eyes closed briefly, the twitch of his lips my only sign that he's not annoyed by my accusation.

"Yeah, Crow O'banian at your service, ma'am." He salutes me with a smirk on his face. The words, along with the action and his stature, is appallingly attractive when it so shouldn't be. I know he's trying to keep things light by joking but shit, he is really handsome.

Shut up, Charlie.

"Does everyone else know now?" I wonder as I watch him watch me.

His eyes are so intense. It feels like he's trying to read between the lines, read my mind, and figure me out all at once, and although the intrusion would usually bother me, with him, I find that maybe I don't mind. Crow has seen so much of me, I don't think he'd run no matter what he saw or found in my mind's depths.

"Yeah, everyone knows. My lot were the ones that helped us get in contact with Liam. It's the only reason I haven't bloody shot him down myself because he helped. I don't trust him, but I dunno, maybe he's not that bad."

I follow suit when Crow sits on the floor with my bag between us.

"Are they the mafia?" I ask, realising after speaking that I categorised a them vs us mentality without meaning too. I also note that I didn't ask if Crow was, but rather they as if he wasn't a part of them but rather a part of us when I suppose he isn't at all.

It makes sense, far more sense than I'd like for it to. Crow's laughter and banterful side makes him seem so at ease but when he's angry, frustrated or even in his own bubble with his thoughts, I've seen how deadly and meticulous he can be.

"Yeah. It's not as bad as it sounds though. I mean, it is," he starts, "but probably not like what you think. My family is normal, they're just like the Cobras, it's just a different brand of Club and bad I guess."

"What do they do? What does it mean to be in the mafia?" I ask, unsure of how any of it works aside from what I've read in books or seen on TV, which I have no doubt is incredibly inaccurate.

He laughs, a hearty laugh as he lets his head fall back, his skin lighting up from the sun's streaming through the cloud and trees.

"It doesn't feel any different being an O'banian in the mafia than it does being a part of the Cobras to be honest, Char. We protect what's ours, do what we need to do, and keep going. That's it." Like it's that simple. I doubt it is as simple as he's making it seem but then again, if he's grown up his entire life living inside of that, then it probably doesn't seem all that strange to him.

"So, what were you doing here?" I'm pretty sure I know the answer. I remember spying, or attempting to spy on my dad's meeting a while ago and hearing that the O'banians usually place a spy in the ranks of any base they planned to merge with.

"My family sent me to see what the Cobras were like, where their values and morals lie, what they could offer us in return for what we could offer them." He offers me the truth, which I appreciate now more than ever.

"So now what? What did you report back?" I ask curiously as I turn to watch him.

"I told them that we're merging," he says with a laugh, as if it's the funniest thing in the world.

"You told them? You have that much power over what happens?" I'm not sure why it seems so shocking that he does. If he's the son of some mafia god then he's bound to have sway.

I attempt to look at Crow as I did the first time I saw him. I remember thinking about how intimidating he was, how large his personality and presence was. I remember noticing so many people cowering under his stare. His personality as I got to know him has allowed me to see him as the teddy bear he really is, but I'm certain he could be just as deadly as any other when needed.

"I didn't really give them a choice to be honest, babe. I've grown to love the Cobras nearly as much as I do you," he says softly as he takes my hand in his and uses his free hand to run his fingers across my palm.

"OK."

"OK? You don't have any more questions?"

"Well, I mean, I'm sure I will at some point but right now I'm just going with the flow, so OK." I nod at him, enjoying his hands in mine.

He gifts me with a small smile that sends my stomach somersaulting.

"I got you something. It's nothing exciting, but I saw it and it made me think of you. Do you want it now?" he asks as he pulls his hands away from mine and goes in his pocket, pulling out a small black box.

"If that's a proposal coming, the answer is no. I'm still pissed at you, at least wait until after you've made me hash browns." I laugh.

"I think you've had plenty of marriage arrangements for a while. I'm not in a rush." He chuckles, holding his hand out for me to take the box.

I take it hesitantly, watching as his eyes show me the nervousness that he's emitting.

"Is it going to make me cry? Because I've cried enough for a while too," I tell him as I feel the smooth box in my hand.

"I hope not, I never know what to do when girls cry. Just open it," he tells me eagerly as he shifts closer to me, moving the bag between us out of the way.

I open the box up slowly, not wanting to rattle or accidentally break whatever is inside. There's a small section of black paper that I move to reveal a necklace. On a black chain with a silver pendant is a necklace with paper inside. Paper covered in words - a segment out of my favourite book that only Crow would know about.

A bright smile takes over as I touch the pendant delicately, lapping up the thoughts of how caring and sweet Crow can be. I've never seen anything like this before, but of course Crow of all people would somehow find something so small and yet meaningful to gift me.

"Do you like it?" he asks nervously as he peers in my direction, his neck craning down to see my face.

"I love it. Thank you," I tell him as I close the lid of the box and smile up at him.

"Is it your dad that runs the O'banians?" I ask suddenly, my earlier idea coming back to me in the silence.

"Yeah, he's the one in charge of our patch, why?" Crow asks, his gaze infiltrating my own suspiciously.

"What's he like?"

"He's pretty chill. I mean, he can be a scary bastard when he wants to be, but he's not that bad really." He laughs lightly, his eyes still watching me as if I'm about to pounce.

"Would you be able to arrange for me to meet him by any chance?"

"I'd love for you to meet my dad knowing that you're mine, but I have a feeling this isn't one of those 'meet the family because we're together' type of dinners, is it?"

"I have an idea I'd like to run by him," I tell him.

"Are you going to tell me this idea of yours?" he asks as he places a hand on my leg and begins caressing it steadily.

"Arrange a meeting with your dad and you can be there to find out."

Fourteen

CHARLIE

I said that I would go to the club today and up until about five minutes ago, I was feeling completely at ease with that thought. Now that I'm standing outside the Club doors, however, I am suddenly feeling like I'm either about to very literally shit myself, cry, or have a complete breakdown. Or maybe all three. Hopefully not at the same time.

Aside from when they've had no choice, Liam nor Crow have left my side once and they're both here now, insisting that everything will be absolutely fine. Liam needs to be interviewed. Again. And I need to get over the built-up fear of being inside of the Club.

"Come on, why don't we spend the afternoon together? After we've done everything we need to here?" Crow asks as he pulls his leather jacket on.

"The three of us?" I ask, confused.

Although neither have left my side, both Crow and Liam have also somehow managed to avoid being with each other all that much. If I'm upstairs, one of them has been with me while the other is downstairs. Usually Liam is the one downstairs. We've hardly had any chance to talk since being home.

We've not managed to speak about anything that happened,

what's going to happen now, or if what did happen was just a case of us both being in a rather sticky situation where we used each other as an outlet for that. I don't think that's the case but until I have the opportunity to ask him what the hell is going on in his mind, I also have absolutely no idea either. He's hardly touched me since being home and though even a few weeks ago, that would have pleased me, I find myself now missing his touch and the comfort I'd become used to from him.

"Yeah, Liam will too, won't you?" Crow asks him, giving him a look that says 'say yes or else' but I don't stop him. If these two could get on, it would make everything so much easier.

"Yeah, course," Liam says as he opens the door in front of us and waves his arm in front of me, signalling for me to go in front.

I stand there transfixed, listening to the music coming from inside for a moment, doubting my ability to overcome this so quickly. But if I don't go in now, will I ever? I have Liam and Crow right by my side. They weren't here last time, and that's why I managed to get taken. They wouldn't let anything happen to me. They won't. I'm safe. I'm ok. Everything will be fine.

I walk inside with Liam and Crow at my side, heading straight towards Ben at the bar. He's the first familiar face that comes into my line of sight. I take hold of that and aim for him. He hasn't noticed me yet, but when I take a seat on one of the bar stools, his head rises and a line of confusion crosses his eyes before a smile lights up his face as he sees me.

"Char! Oh, bloody hell, girl, I haven't seen you in forever," he says as he opens the flap of the bar, walks through, and comes to give me a hug.

Ben is one of Gray's usual hookups. Not as though he's told me that, but I've noticed the way that Ben looks at him and very conveniently gets to finish work and follow Gray to one of the rooms here and then comes back dishevelled and messy. Gray thinks I don't notice these things, but I most definitely do. Ben is only a few inches taller than me, maybe 5'10 at a guess, has a slim build and no hair on his face. He has dark, nearly black eyes and hair to match that goes in every which direction.

"Oh, you're looking good, babe! You want a drink?" he asks as he lets me go, looking at me once more with a smile before going back behind the bar and waiting eagerly for my order.

"Yeah, I'll just have an orange juice please. Way too early for the harder stuff," I joke as he laughs and takes Liam's and Crow's orders before collecting our drinks.

"So, what are you doing here? Alice isn't around today, but she'll be back in tomorrow if you were looking for her," He tells me as he slides my drink over the counter and waves away the notes that Liam offers him.

"No, Liam and Crow have got a meeting and are busy this afternoon, so I thought I'd stop by with them instead of waiting at home on my own. Is Dad around?" I ask as I glance around and see many other familiar faces but not my dad's. He said he was going to work early this morning but that didn't necessarily mean that he was here.

"Yeah, he's in one of the meeting rooms. Probably waiting for you lot. Are you late?" he wonders with a wag of his eyebrows.

"I don't actually know," I tell him with a small laugh as I look towards Liam. "Are we?"

He looks at the clock above Ben's head before turning to me with a smirk. "Yep. Half an hour late, as it happens."

"Why the hell didn't you tell me? Dad's gonna go bloody crazy. Come on," I tell him as I grab his arm and yank him towards the doors to the meeting rooms.

"I'll see you later, Ben!" I shout back at him as I walk off while dragging Liam.

"There's no rush. You wanted to do your hair," he tells me as he swipes my hand away, straightens himself, and then grabs my hand again.

"I could have just put it in a bobble if I knew we were on a time crunch," I hiss out.

"Nah, he's right, your dad won't care," Crow tells me as he catches up with us and takes my other side.

"Do you even know my dad?" I ask, exasperated. "He will most definitely care." I huff out as I continue plodding along towards the meeting rooms.

I pull to a stop outside the door I can hear conversation coming from while I wait for a very slow Liam and Crow. They seriously could not take any longer if they tried. They both have such confident walks, I realise as I watch them with agitation filling my face. If nothing else, speeding ahead gives me a moment to take in the absolute god given beauty of them. Now that I'm looking at them standing side by side, I realise how similar they are. I've never thought about it or noticed it before but they both have buzz cuts - well, they did, Crows has grown out a bit since but Liam's is still short. Their hair is only a few shades apart from one another and their builds are also eerily similar aside from Liam being maybe three inches or so taller than Crow.

"You look like you're eye fucking us, princess," Crow tells me as he staggers towards me with a smirk on his face.

"I was most definitely not doing that," I tell him with a terrible hair flick as I turn around, mortified because I absolutely was doing exactly that.

"You look like one of those popular girls when you flick your hair like that." Crow laughs as he loops his arm around my shoulders and kisses the side of my head.

"I do not, at all. I look cool and dignified when I flick my hair," I tell him even though I know for a fact that I am lying through my teeth.

"You really do. You know that blonde one in Mean Girls that you used to make me watch? Her." Liam joins in with a smirk on his face.

"Yeah, man, that's the one!" Crow laughs, his head falling back as he does.

I whack Crow in the stomach lightly in an attempt to either hurt him or shut him up.

"Are you done picking on me now? Are we going in or not?"

"We're still ten minutes early, there's no need to rush," Liam tells me as he checks the time on his phone and shows it to me.

"It's three o'clock. I thought you said we were half an hour late?" I ask, confused.

"I did. I lied. No one's supposed to be meeting us until ten past. I just knew you hate being late and I know your dad likes it even less, so I thought if I distracted you then you wouldn't worry as much about being here and walking down the hall," he tells me simply, with the most 'duh' expression ever, as if I should have known something so seemingly obvious.

I look at him, completely dumbfounded at the thought that went into him doing something so simple that helped so much. He is right. I hadn't thought about my clammy hands, my erratically beating heart, or the harsh breaths that were coming out of me even once since he mentioned us being late.

"Did you know about this?" I ask Crow.

"Well, no, but I figured it out when he told you we were late when I knew damn well that we were not and then he kept smirking at you so I put two and two together and made eleven point seven, so yeah, I knew before you," he tells me with a nod of his head as if everyone should understand his maths.

A smile creeps up on my face as I glance between them both.

"Are you lot coming in or just standing in the hall all damn day?" I hear Tins gruff voice shout from inside the room. The door is open slightly, his voice loud enough to echo and be heard down the hall.

"We're coming now, chill ya beans, jeez," Crow says as he saunters inside and takes a seat at the table, totally unbothered by Tin's huffing and puffing. One thing about Tin is that he hates waiting. He likes to be busy all of the time, so if he's got something to do, he likes to get it over and done with so that he can move onto his next task.

I'm sat between Liam and Crow with my dad, Tin, and Mal sat opposite us. Mal is very introverted and prefers to spend his time away from others, but in these situations, he's the only one that's had any genuine history in his life with questioning, interviews, and psychology. He was a police officer with a psychology degree so although this isn't anything official, he knows how to conduct himself a lot better than anyone else my dad could have asked in the Cobras.

"Right, everyone here? Let's move on. Liam. Mal, let's go," Tin says pointedly as he nods in Liam's direction.

"We've gone over everything we need to. I just have a few questions for you, and then we'll talk among the three of us and get back to you with an official decision."

Liam nods, looking completely unphased. I'm not sure that Liam wants this life anymore. I know that he adores the Cobras and the men within, but that doesn't change the fact that after everything he's endured, I'm sure he'd prefer a peaceful life away from the chaos of club life or at least a lesser part in the Cobras that doesn't demand as much of him.

"Are you happy for me to proceed with Crow and Charlie here? Some of the questions are of a rather intimate nature," Mal says delicately.

Liam avoids my eyes but looks past me at Crow, who gives him a tentative smile. Crow may be the joker but he has a bigger heart than most people I know. He's one of the least judgmental people ever, but I'd also understand if Liam doesn't want me or Crow to be here to listen to whatever it is that needs to be spoken about.

"It's fine. Go on," Liam instructs Mal, who opens up the stack of papers in front of him.

"The first question was in relation to your father. You said that he has a vendetta against you and with the evidence you've given, we have reason to believe you. What I want to know is if you feel he has the ability to take down the Cobras with the assets he has. Our main concern here is the Club and those within it. This isn't a question so much about your character but rather what your father is capable of."

"He's got intel coming from most areas of law enforcement and is friends with more people that can help him than I care to know about. Between his connections and his men, I have no doubt that if he came while the Cobras were unprepared, he could annihilate us all." Liam says it with so much nonchalance that it terrifies me. I know that he's not a particularly dramatic person. If he genuinely thinks that his father and his men could take down the Cobras, I'm certain he's right.

My dad's jaw tics as Tin huffs, but none of them make a move to speak. Mal continues.

"You said that your main weakness, the one way he'd be able to get to you, would be through Charlie. Is that correct?"

"Yes."

"Why is it that she is your weakness over anyone else in your life?"

"Because I love her." My eyes practically bug out of my skull at hearing him say the words so relaxed, as if he's saying 'duh - obviously' without saying it at all.

"And in what way do you love her?" my dad asks as he leans forward over the table and towards us.

I don't meet his eyes when he speaks, though even if I wanted to I couldn't, his eyes are glued on Liam's.

"In a very different way to the way you lot love her." He chuckles deeply, so calm and confident in his declaration.

My dad's jaw clenched and releases as he continues, "Make it clear for me here, mate, so that I'm not stuck making assumptions. In what way do you love my daughter?" Oh Jesus, this is not going well. The frustration is brimming in my father's eyes.

"In exactly the way you don't want me to. I love her so

much that I want to spend every single fucking second with her, so much that I'd happily live my life with her, so much that I'm willing to put up with him for her too." He rushes out with a smirk as he points his head in Crow's direction.

"Oh thanks, make it sound like I'm a fucking side piece, why don't you? I'm the OG, you're the bloody late comer," Crow huffs out with a roll of his eyes.

"You're telling me that you want to be with my daughter?" my dad asks, surprisingly calm in his demeanour. I mean, he looks understandably tense but overall he doesn't look like he's about to hurt Liam too badly. He doesn't look like he wants to maim him, you know? That's good.

"What if we don't trust you? What do you plan to do then? Go back to your father?" Tin asks, completely ignoring Liam and my dad's dispute.

"Why are we moving on? I'm not done!" my dad exclaims, his hands in the air as he looks at Tin in shock.

"Does no one else care that my best friend wants to be with my fucking daughter?"

"Not really. He's a dickhead, but he ain't a bad man and you know it. Moving on," Tin says, ever the one to not want unnecessary chatter, unless it's from me or Gray, who seem to get away with it of course. The positives of being like one of his own children to him.

"We're talking about this later. Don't be thinking you're staying in her room anymore," my dad says, his eyes not leaving Liam.

"What, so you'll let him stay with her but not me? You've known me for years," Liam argues.

"He's earned my trust unlike some," my dad hisses out, though I can tell his anger is waning.

"He's a fucking undercover O'banian!"

"Well, that's fucking rude," Crow butts in.

"OK, how about we move on like Tin said? I don't think we're going to achieve anything positive by carrying on this conversation right now," I interrupt, knowing that despite my father slowly calming that the more we talk about it, the more his wrath will grow again.

My dad and Liam nod their heads, not looking at each other as Tin and Mal continue firing questions at Liam.

Once the initial disagreements are over with, so too are the questions rather quickly.

It doesn't take long before we're out of the Club house and left alone again. Since both Liam and Crow aren't in the best of moods after the meeting, my wonderful idea is to let them pick what we do for the afternoon.

Crow chooses go-karting or paintballing while Liam picks the cinema or hiking. Complete opposite choices of course. They're crazily similar sight wise and yet their personalities can't be more different.

I end up deciding on something completely different. We go to the wildlife park. I am your typical young woman that adores animals, coos at every newborn baby I see, no matter what form it is in - human or animal. Plus, my decision means that they can't argue over who gets to pick what we do.

Fifteen

CHARLIE

After spending the afternoon with Crow and Liam, I feel like a weight has been lifted from me. Joking and messing around with them makes me realise just how much I'd missed being myself without the chaos. Crow and I were usually together 24/7 so to be away from each other for weeks felt like years, at least in my mind.

"You alright, darlin'? I got chippy!" my dad shouts as he comes through the front door.

"You know I love you, don't you?" I ask with a laugh as I get up to retrieve some cutlery and drinks for us.

"We eating in the lounge, Charlie?" he asks, though I have no idea why since he's already settled himself on the sofa and opened up his food.

"I want to have a chat," he tells me.

I lower myself to sit next to him. Crow and Liam said they had business to take care of at the Club, but that they'll be here soon.

"Just wait a second, you knew I was getting knives and forks, you idiot. You're worse than a child." I scoff, handing him a napkin from beside me as well as his cutlery.

"And you're like a bloody mother hen, my girl," he says laughing.

I smirk at his comment, knowing full well that it's true. These men would never survive if it weren't for me.

I dig into the chips, sausage and gravy he'd got me - my absolute favourite takeaway meal.

We eat in silence for a while, with just the tv as background noise. I soon finish up and chuck the plastic container in the bin and place the cutlery into the sink.

"So, what is it you want to talk about?" I ask as I walk back in to sit down again.

The doorbell goes before Dad has a chance to say anything. I roll my eyes at our uninvited visitor's terrible timing.

"I'll grab it." Dad jumps up from next to me and catapults to the door.

"Alright, old man?" Liam.

I can hear them muttering something to one another, but not their words.

Dad follows Liam and Crow into the lounge. Liam takes the seat next to me, Crow sitting on the arm of the chair, whilst Dad takes his seat in the corner.

Liam gives me a pointed look, but I have no idea what it's supposed to mean so I don't respond with my voice or my actions, turning to face Dad.

"They're gonna stay for this conversation, Charl," Dad says. He seems tense, which makes me nervous. He is sat upright, which makes a change for him since he's usually laid back in the comfiest chair we own. His hands are knitted together too, fiddling with the cutlery still in his hand.

I look towards Liam and Crow for any indication of what's going on, but neither of them are looking at me. Liam shakes his head slightly as if in answer to me though. No? Don't ask. Is that what he's trying to say?

"So, what is it that's got you all twisted up?" I ask, concerned more than curious seeing the state of the three men.

"You know you had that doctor's appointment a while back?"

"Yeah, is something wrong?" I wonder.

"No, not physically. No one's ill." Well, that's a start. He's staring at the ground as he speaks though. Something is wrong.

I nod at him to let him know I heard. Waiting for him to continue.

"I don't really know where to start to be honest with you, darlin'," he explains. He looks up at me this time with a weak smile that I return, encouraging him to continue.

"You know all about your mum, about what she was like when we were together." My mind reels, wondering why on earth she had anything to do with this. I do know though. I've been told by so many people how awful she was to him.

I don't remember much about her, but I hear enough and remember her golden hair and her hard, green eyes refusing to ever play with me or cuddle me. She didn't want me, but Dad did. He took over when she disappeared. I've had a better life with him and without a mum than I would have had if she had stuck around. Considering what she'd recently let her only two children witness and go through, I have no doubt about the horrendous stories I've been told of her over the years.

"She cheated on me a lot throughout the years." I already knew this, but say nothing, waiting for him to continue. "I had a tip off a few months ago, a random letter in the post telling me that you weren't mine."

A letter in the post? Who the hell would come up with something like that? There are always rumours about everyone in life. Rumours and speculations are what create half the things the world talks about, but to tell a man their daughter isn't theirs eighteen years after said daughter is born, it just baffles me.

"But I am though. We're exactly the same," I say with a light laugh. If this is what is worrying him then he is just being silly. Our personalities are exactly the same.

"We like our tea the same way, we both love hash browns, we can both shoot better than this dead shot over here," I say, jerking my thumb towards Liam. "We practically have identical personalities, Dad," I say with a chuckle.

"You're right. We're very similar, but do you realise what you just said, darlin'?" I think back to the words I used but don't understand what he's referring to.

"They're all learned habits, Charlie. All things that anyone would grow up being if they were brought up by me. You've always been a daddy's girl, followed me, copied me. You wanted to be just like me, and you are." I realise then what he meant.

I always thought we looked alike too, but now that I'm looking at him, I understood it.

Our hair and eye colours are different. Our face shapes are complete opposites, as well as our individual features. I don't have any of his physical features. His pitch-black hair in comparison to my mousy brown doesn't match. My nose is annoyingly small in comparison to his prominent one. My lips are full and plump whereas his are thin and small. Small differences but differences all the same.

"I could have just taken after Mum instead of you though," I say hesitantly.

It's true. We don't have pictures of her around, not because my dad doesn't want to or wouldn't, but because I've never been that interested in her. I've been told so much about her that's negative, and the small memories I do have of her are never anything good either, so neither of us really see the point. So many people look like one parent and not the other. Crow showed me pictures of his parents and he looks identical to his dad, but nothing like his mum.

"I contacted a man I knew your mum was sleeping with at the time we were together, around the time you were conceived. I explained the situation and he was willing to give me a DNA sample so that we could compare it in case it came to it." I shake my head, standing.

A man? What man? A DNA sample. My mind works at a mile a minute, repeating Dads words back to myself. The doctor. He took a swab from inside my mouth. I knew that was a bit strange at the time but didn't think much of it. Why didn't he tell me? Why did no one mention it when this letter arrived?

I answer my own question before I even get a chance to ask. My dad does everything within his power to avoid me having any stress in my life, any worries or problems. He wouldn't want to worry me. That's why he wouldn't have told me.

"The doctor did the test," I state, feeling like my mind is spinning in circles but realising when Crow's arms stop me that it's not my mind but me slowly spinning in circles.

I stop abruptly and look up to Liam's fallen face.

Neither he nor Crow would look so distraught if I was my dad's daughter. My dad wouldn't look so devastated if I was his.

They'd be overjoyed. Happy. Truth was, they probably wouldn't even mention it or, if they did, they wouldn't look as concerned as they did now. My dad's face is not that of a happy man.

"This man you got the samples from, do they-" I can't say it.

"They match yours. He's your biological father. I'm not." My dad's face falls even more, and I can feel my eyebrows knitting together.

No. No. No, this is not happening. Absolutely not. I feel my head shaking again, wishing more than anything that I could shake this whole conversation away. Dad isn't my dad? But he is. He is. My mind can't process the mess that's happening right in front of me, and I find myself looking at my dad, checking his face for a smile, a smirk to tell me that this is some sick joke. But he's not smiling, his lips aren't lifted. He's crying.

I'm still as a statue. Unable to move. My mind seems to freeze in place, incapable of understanding what I'm being told.

Why is Dad crying? Am I crying? I lift a hand to my face to

feel my cheeks, but there's no water. No tears. I'm not crying. Dad's crying.

I move away from Liam's arms and kneel in front of my dad, gently tearing his hands away from his tear-stained face.

"I'm so fucking sorry, Charlie," he cries.

"Why are you sorry? Just because we don't have the same DNA, it doesn't mean you're not my dad, you bloody idiot," I say with a laugh.

I might cry later, but I can't handle dad being upset, being torn apart. I need to help him now. He's my dad. He read me stories as a child, and rocked me to sleep. He hand-fed me food when I was being a lazy toddler, and he taught me the truth about life. He taught me how to live, how to take care of myself. My dad lifted me and kissed me when I fell and grazed my knee so many times whilst learning to ride a bike. He's my dad, and now my dad is upset. My poor dad is in tears, and I have no idea what I need to do to make him feel better, the way he's made me feel better so many times throughout my life. He needs me. He needs reassurance.

"Come here, you big baby," I say as I stand up and pull him into a hug. This is how it was at the start after what happened. Me trying to take his sorrow and sadness away. He's strong but sometimes he needs help, and that's ok. I need to help him now and think later.

"You're such a good woman. I'm supposed to be the one consoling you, and here you are comforting me. You're too good, I should have known sooner," he says with a disgruntled sigh as he pulls away from my embrace.

"Well, I mean I am pretty amazing," I tell him, "but like you said, that's learned, so it's gotta be from you." I shove his arm lightly before tucking myself back into his arms.

He needs me to be his baby girl right now. He needs to know I'm his, so I let myself get lost in my dad's arms.

"I love you so much, you know that, don't you, darlin'?" he mutters into my hair.

"I know. I love you too, you fool," I say with a chuckle.

He pulls back and lets me go, looking at me like he always has. Like I'm still a tiny little baby he still needs to look after.

"His name is David Bancroft. He didn't know about you until I explained. He got the results at the same time as me. He's desperate to meet you, but I asked for a few days so that you can decide. I hate to say it, but he does seem like a good guy, darlin'." He rubs the back of his neck in an awkward gesture of uncertainty.

"I'll meet him, but I'm doing it here. I hope you didn't think you could get rid of me that easily," I say with a smile.

"Wait, what about Gray? He really does look just like you," I say as I think of the physical similarities between the two of them.

Gray's been absent more than he's been here since we got back. I've not wanted to push him, so I've done my best to let him experience life again in whatever way he sees fit.

"Yeah, he's mine, and he knows about this. He didn't want you to feel overwhelmed so he went to work," my dad says with a sad smile.

We spend the rest of the night talking things through, my dad explaining and me comforting him whilst Liam and Crow comfort me.

I don't want to imagine anyone else being my dad. I can't imagine anyone else doing a better job than what my dad's done. I'm not always a grateful daughter, but I do my best to always be a loving one. I think I sometimes forget or perhaps just don't realise how hard it's been for my dad, bringing up a daughter on his own alongside trying to work, run a club, and earn money. He's given up so much for me, and now to find out that it was all for a daughter that isn't biologically his – I'm not surprised he's so upset.

The logical part of me knows my next thoughts aren't true, but I can't help but wonder if perhaps he feels differently about me now that he knows our DNA isn't shared, if maybe that's why he's so devastated because knowing I'm not biologically his has made the love he's always showered me with diminish some.

Liam hardly says a word, not wanting to interrupt I assume, but he keeps his arms on me throughout the night, whether that be by placing his hand on my back, locking our hands together, or having his arm around my shoulder. He is making it known that he is there when I am ready, and I appreciate that.

Crow, unlike the brooding Liam, jumps in with jokes and banter to ease any tension that arises when certain topics are brought up. His naturally charming and humorous nature serves to be something I'm beyond grateful for.

They're the perfect mixture of everything I need, I realise.

Sixteen

CHARLIE

"He's not your dad? Holy shit!" Alice huffs out as she sits back, eyes wide, and takes a sip of the wine in her hand.

"Yup, tell me about it. I thought my head was full on going to explode," I say with a forced laugh. If I don't laugh, I'll cry, right?

"Wait, is your real dad hot? Matt's hot," Kira butts in as she watches me eagerly.

"He is definitely not hot. He's old enough to be your dad." Liam laughs as he shakes his head at Kira.

"So are you, but you're still hot." Kira is thirteen. Thirteen.

"Kira, no! You can't say stuff like that to grown-ass men," Alice chastises her as she rubs a hand over her forehead and eyes.

"Well, I just did, so boo-hoo, baby," she says as she glares mockingly at Alice.

She has more sass than anyone I know. More confidence. More arrogance and more insanity, but she's also the coolest thirteen-year-old you'll ever meet too.

"What about me? Why am I being left out? My mum always told me I was handsome," Crow says as he fakes a pout and flutters his lashes at us all, causing a laugh to break out between me, Alice, and Kira.

"Why are you all laughing? I'm bloody gorgeous," he informs us as he looks around at us all with a crooked brow and confusion marring his beautiful face.

"You're hot, too, don't worry," I tell him as a giggle escapes while I pat his leg.

"It's the older men. The girls dig it," Liam tells him, his face as confused as Crow's.

"First of all, no one says dig it anymore, which just shows exactly how old you are. Secondly, you're not that old. Third, how the fuck old are you?" Kira asks Liam as she leans in closer.

"Will you stop swearing? You've literally just become a teenager, you do not need to be saying that kind of stuff," Alice says as she takes another large gulp of her wine.

I have no idea how she does this alone. No parents or family, and although the Cobras and a few neighbours help her with Kira, I genuinely can't understand how someone so young can cope with the responsibility alone. I need to make sure to come around and help more often. Not as though I do much to help, but just being there is more than their own family offers.

"I'm thirty-two. Not that old, but far too old for you to even be joking about, kid. Stop giving your sister a damn heart attack, will you? It'll upset Char and then I'll have to take your Haribo off you," Liam threatens as Kira looks mortified and hugs her packet of sweets closer to her chest.

"Jeez, that's harsh! I'll be good, ugh. Men," she mutters as she slides another sweet into her mouth while glaring at Liam.

"How did things go with you and Edgar? Dad said you haven't seen him for a while."

I'm not sure how willing she is to talk about him but considering she was practically gushing over him the last time I'd spoke to her before I was taken, I'll bet that she isn't over him as much as she probably wants everyone to think.

"She's being difficult. He has flowers, a note, and different snacks delivered here every single day. She won't even open any of them," Kira tells us, rolling her eyes at her sister - the consequence of which is a whack on her arm from Alice.

"It's not that simple," Alice tells me, shaking her head.

I wait, sensing there's more she wants to say.

"At the start, I was worried that he had something to do with your disappearance and then I realised when he helped so much that he can't have, but I don't think it's really that at all. I think I'm just terrified of him leaving. Kira and I both got so attached to him after just a few days, imagine a month or a year and then him leaving us," she says quietly. Kira's face falls as well, as if thinking about that and how much it would hurt.

Considering the way they've been abandoned before, I can see why, but Alice particularly has worries.

"I know that logically you must know this, but I'm going to say it anyway. If you don't let anyone in enough to let them hurt you, you'll miss out on some of the best opportunities in the world. Not just in a romantic sense but in so many other ways too. Sometimes you have to risk being hurt and just hope for the best instead," I tell her, watching as she nods at me softly.

Alice is one of the brightest people I know, with a personality to match, but since I've been back, I've noticed that the flame burning inside of her seems to have diminished. I thought that maybe Edgar had hurt her in some way and she was trying to get over him, but it seems she's the one that broke it off despite not wanting to get over him. I can't say I'm particularly keen on the man, considering my past and the stories I've been told about him, but if someone as lively and lovely as Alice got to know and appreciate him for who he is then who am I to judge? Especially considering my current predicament with the two men sitting beside me. Someone even more traumatised and hurt than I am and another man that lied from the first day I met him.

"If it's any consolation, I did a lot of research on everyone, including him before joining the Cobras, and I can safely say without giving his whole life away that he doesn't attach himself to anyone unless they mean a lot to him. He's not close to many people but the people he is close with get the fiercest form of protection and love from him. He doesn't leave anyone," Crow says, his usually bashful and humorous tone now gone, giving way for the sensible and caring side of him that I adore just as much.

I think I knew; I must have known that Crow did his research before joining us, but what I didn't think about was him potentially knowing a lot more about all of us than we perhaps realised. He'd never, so far as I know, used information about anyone against them and yet I have a feeling that he knows enough that he could if he ever needs to.

"I told you he won't just leave," Kira murmurs to Alice.

I watch as the two sisters smile at one another, Alice's eyes looking lighter and filled with promise as she takes Kira's hand in hers.

Seventeen

CROW

She's nervous. I can't figure out if she's nervous because she's meeting my family, nervous because she's meeting the head of the Irish Mafia, or nervous because she's about to ask for something that I really hope I've guessed wrong. I take her hand, relishing in the way she automatically brings her body closer to mine for comfort. I press my body into hers, bringing her head to my chest as I breathe in the fresh ocean scent of her. Her body taught against mine does unexplainable things to me, setting the very rarely placed dick in my pants into overdrive.

Her arms wrap around me, her head beneath my chin, fitting perfectly in the space between my neck and chest. She folds her body into mine further, my cock over the soft curves of her stomach. Fuck, she feels nice. I could happily live the rest of my days with her body against mine.

Shut the fuck up, Crow.

You do not need a boner right now.

I let her hold on for another moment before gently pulling away from her, watching as Liam walks up from behind her towards us.

He gives me a nod, a knowing grin, and juts his head

towards the door behind me. My family are in a hotel suite, the door of which is currently behind me.

"Whatever this is, Char, it can wait, we don't have to do this now," I tell her, hoping that she understands, that she knows what I'm trying to say when I'm not even sure myself half the time.

"Just stay close, both of you," she tells us as Liam puts his hand on her lower back and guides her towards the door.

I've spent so long worrying about her that I hadn't even considered that this would be the first time I'd seen my family since I began the infiltration of the Cobras. I spoke to them constantly; Charlie had heard me on the phone to them a lot. Despite what everyone seems to think, we are way more average than you'd assume. You know, give or take a few deaths, murders and wars here and there obviously.

"You ready?" I ask her as I take her face in my hands and place a kiss on her forehead. God, she's fucking beautiful. She makes me want to pray to a deity I've never believed in just to keep her by my side for eternity. I'll happily fucking burn in hell for as long as needed so long as I get to her at the end of it.

She nods, throws a smile that I know damn well is filled with fake confidence my way, and then proceeds to push me towards the door.

Right. OK. It'll be fine.

There's not a single part of me that is worried about my family not liking her or her not liking them, even though I'm sure that's got to have been something that has crossed her mind. Despite the way she often sees herself, she's one of the most self-aware and selfless people I've ever met. I mean, how often do you meet someone that can forgive the guy that set her up? Even thinking about Victor makes me want to fucking pummel him. I shake thoughts of the stupid fucker away and pull myself towards the door.

I knock on the door once, not even getting a second rap on the wood in before it's sprung open, revealing my mum.

"Oh, my baby boy!" She squeals as she pulls me into her embrace and holds my head down to her level while squeezing me with all of her might.

I might be a grown ass man, but I'm not going to lie and say that my mum's hugs aren't the best. The best familial hugs at least. Char gets top spot for all other types of hugs.

"Let him up, Mary, no one else will get a look in if you don't." My dad huffs from behind her.

"He's my son, and I'll damn well hug him as much as I want, thank you very much!" she sasses back as she squeezes me some more.

My mum's a little shorter than Charlie and small in build, but her sass and attitude definitely make up for it. She lets me go, her eyes finding Charlie, and I watch in awe as her face lights up.

"Oh, look at you! You are just beautiful, sweet pea!" my mum gushes as she rushes over to Charlie and takes her in her arms.

Char looks momentarily panicked before relaxing a little and awkwardly hugging my mum back. Liam seems about as astounded as Char is, and I can't help but laugh at that. Talk about a fish out of water and you've got Liam - a man who looks pretty uncomfortable right now. Can't say I blame him. He's in uncharted territory.

My dad gives me a hug, patting me on the back and ruffling my hair a little before shaking Liam's hand and introducing himself to Charlie.

"So, I hear you wanted a chat with me, Charlie girl. Shall we get to it?" he asks gruffly.

"Yes, please. I really appreciate you coming all this way," she tells him, her voice taking on that of a professional as she talks to my dad.

She may not have been involved with the Cobras dealings, but she definitely gets the confidence, even if it is a show, from her dad. I've watched him in the most intense and intimidating situations act cool and collected, and that's exactly how Char appears despite the hidden terror and nerves I know she's feeling. I have a feeling I know what's coming and even though a part of me is dreading it, I also can't be more proud of what she's willing and able to overcome to ask for something so outrageously out there.

"Well, I needed to see this lad you've got hooked on you, it's not a completely selfless trip," my dad says with a smile as my mum takes his arm and leads him to the two sofas facing one another. There's a glass coffee table between them that my dad collects his drink from before taking a seat and encouraging Char to take a seat on the sofa opposite him.

I grab a chair from the table and sit next to her, letting Liam take her other side on the sofa.

"I'm not sure I'd say he's hooked." Char laughs while looking at me with a smile that makes her eyes look even brighter. Fuck, her smile kills me every time. I need to take more pictures of her smiling. Not right now, though, shut up, Crow.

"Oh, he definitely is. Did you know that he talks about you every single time we speak?" Zak, my youngest brother, says as he walks in from an adjoining room. He gives a quick fist bump before taking a chair and sits by us.

Zak took after our mum more than Coran, my oldest brother, or I did. Zak is taller than me by maybe an inch or two but more slender too. He has more of a swimmer or a runner's body, with his light hair matching my mums. Coran and I both look much more like our dad with darker hair, more natural muscle as well as our father's obsession with tattoos. Zak always says he wants a tattoo or two, but I don't think he'll ever get one. He's smart, like stupidly smart, and says he doesn't understand the enjoyment from causing yourself pain.

"You alright, man? Where's Coran?" I ask, knowing that my parents wouldn't have come for too long without him. He and my dad are the ones in charge of the business side of things and are constantly in meetings together online, over the phone or in person, always consulting one another.

"We've left him at home to take care of things while we're here. He'll be taking over when I retire so it's about time he has the chance to prove himself without my help," my dad says, his hands gripping onto the glass of what I've got to assume is whiskey in his hand.

So, this is a business meeting, I realise. My dad rarely drinks but anytime he's in a business meeting, he has whiskey.

"He'll do just fine, I don't know why you insist on acting like he won't," my mum scolds him with a light whack to his shoulder as she sits next to him.

"I didn't say he wouldn't do just fine," he objects, rolling his eyes in exasperation at her.

My mum glares at him a little more before turning her gaze back on Charlie.

"So, what can we do for you, dear?" she asks as she leans forward in anticipation.

I watch Char for any clues or worry emitting from her, but she's the picture of confidence and grace as she smiles kindly at my mum.

"Well, as it happens, I'm after your official support," she starts, and I'm thinking nothing other than fuck no as she continues, "I'd like to run for President of the Cobras."

There's absolute silence as my father's lip twitches into a smile he tries to hide and my mother's eyes light up as if it's the best thing she's ever heard. Zak doesn't look surprised in the least and, as I look at Liam, he's doing nothing other than glaring daggers at Charlie's head. OK, great. Going well. No problems here.

Hey, God. If you're up there, I'd appreciate it if you could come down and just re-wire Char's brain for a super teeny tiny second so that she changes her mind. Cheers, mate.

I don't want to make her feel like I'm disrespecting her, but I also want to rip her off the sofa, drag her home, and not let her out ever again. How Tamlin of me. She told me about him, one of her redeemable book boyfriends. I genuinely think she prefers the men in books to me half the time but then again, they're made by women for women most of the time so who can blame her?

Back to the present, please, Crow.

Right.

"Why do you want to do that?" my dad asks her, his face clearing of emotion though from the small twitch of his brow, I know he's already made his decision. Fuck.

"It's either me or one other contender. A man from The Laidens that, from what I've been told, will run it to the ground. The Cobras are my family and I want to protect them in the same way that they've always tried to protect me. I want things to be as legal as possible, for them to be a part of society rather than be estranged from it. I want them to be a part of the local community that people feel they can come to if they need help, and I want future generations to have what I've had from them," she says as she lets out a breath, sits a little taller, and straightens her shoulders as she waits for my dad to say something.

Well, shit. I thought she was going to suggest that I take over the Cobras and I was worried that I'd have to ever so kindly refuse, but if this is the way she wants it to go, that includes a lot of change. But if anyone's capable of enforcing it, it's her. She's so much stronger than she realises. Her stubborn streak is made of iron, her mind made of tougher stuff than I've got in me, and her will and wit capable of anything. But she will need help. A lot of it. And there's no one else I'd trust to help her aside from myself.

Well, fuck. Here we go.

"I'd like to rescind my title and offer myself as a second for Charlie in the Cobras. I want to make the transition permanent and official," I tell my dad. I watch as my mother's face lights up even more, my dad smirks, and Zak rolls his eyes at me.

"You have that much trust in her or are you blinded by love?" my dad asks me after another moment of silence.

"It's got nothing to do with love. I believe in everything Charlie wants to do, and I want to help her achieve it, which I can't officially do unless my title is taken from me." It's the way it works in the Irish Mafia. You can't be an O'banian and a Cobra.

My dad looks between us, his gaze indecisive and curious.

"You'd be willing to give up your future for this?" my dad asks me.

I nod my head, not needing to expand on it. Charlie's eyes find mine as she gives me a gentle and tentative smile.

"Very well then. You both have my full support. When you become the Cobras President, I expect a merge as well, and so long as you're OK with that happening then Crow needn't give up his title."

"Can we have dinner now? I need a proper catch up with you all, and I want to get to know this handsome little so and so a bit better," my mum says as she wiggles her eyebrows at Liam. Ew. What the fuck is wrong with her? I take everything good back that I've ever said about my mum. Even worse is Liam lapping up the attention and Charlie finding it hilarious. Brilliant. Fucking brilliant.

~

"Was anyone going to tell me about this plan before you set it in motion?" Liam asks, frustrated as we walk back down the hall towards the entrance of the hotel.

"Not really, no," Charlie says dismissively as she does something on her phone. An abrupt laugh leaves me at her tone. She sounds like she's in charge already, though I suppose between the three of us, she is in charge. She knows well that both of us will do anything she says.

"Excuse me, I'm technically still the Cobras President, and

what about your dad?" he asks, exasperated as he stares at her in horror.

"I'm texting him right now, and not for long you're not," she tells him with a sly grin and a condescending pat to his shoulder before she continues walking onward.

"Have you heard this?" Liam asks me as if I'm not finding the situation the most hilarious thing I've ever witnessed.

"Come on, we're going to see the Devils Dealers now. I don't want to be late." Char whistles through to us and clicks her fingers at us impatiently.

"We're going where?" I ask, confused. She cannot surely mean we're asking them for support as well. They hate us.

"Edgar said he'll help us if I put a good word in for him with Alice. I've already told her, I'm not lying to her about it but I also do think he's actually good for her," she says simply. Right. Right, sure.

"And what are we? Just your bodyguards?" Liam asks.

"Pretty much. Come on, my pretty little bodyguards, let's go. Stop being drama queens and move your butts, please. We're on a tight schedule."

Eighteen

CHARLIE

"You need to be quicker at dipping out from under me. You're tiny in comparison to him and if he catches you, you're pretty much done for, Char. The only way you're going to win this is if you can avoid him, wear him out, and then throw a sucker punch his way when he's not expecting it," Crow tells me as he helps me up from the floor again and begins circling me once more.

We've been at it for hours, with Liam watching and instructing from the sidelines, and although as we've already determined I can throw a decent punch, if I'm caught, I'm dead. Well, as good as.

The meeting with the Devils Dealers went as well as expected. With Alice, and therefore Edgar's support, we could potentially have their help. Maybe.

"I need to take a break, I'm dying over here," I tell them as I use the towel on the bench to wipe over my sweat-covered face. I have no doubt that my face is currently as red as a tomato but with how exhausted my limbs feel, I couldn't care less.

"You don't have time for a break. We have very little time to get you ready, and I'm not watching you get beat up so you need to figure out your shit and do it," Liam tells me harshly from the sidelines. I know he's just worried, and I know that I probably need the tough love he's currently throwing my way, but shit, a breather would be nice.

"Fine. Once more and then I'm done for the day," I tell them both as I attempt to shake the exhaustion from my body and stand upright again in front of Crow.

He watches me, his eyes penetrating my every move as we circle each other.

In a split second that I very nearly miss, he comes running towards me. I skirt under his arms as they reach out towards me and grab his ankle, lifting it from behind him and spin around as he lands on the floor beneath me. I jump on his back, bring his hands behind his back and smile triumphantly up at Liam.

"That's once. Do it again. Good job though, baby," he says sweetly. Butterflies flit through my stomach at the praise.

"Wanna let me up now, princess, or am I flipping you over?" Crow asks from below.

I get off his back and run my hands down my now crumpled clothes as they practically stick to me.

"I seriously need a shower. This is gross," I tell no one in particular as I peel off Liam's shirt so that it's just my sports bra underneath on display.

"Who are they from?" Crow asks as he juts his head towards my stomach. It's only now that I am realising that he hasn't seen the rest of my body since I've been home. He hasn't seen the scars littering my skin.

"Matt and Danny," I answer simply, not wanting to get into a conversation about it. The anger and fury in his eyes shock me, but he says no more as his jaw tics and his teeth grind one another.

"Stop, I'm fine," I tell him, my hands on his jaw as I lay a light kiss on his chin.

"Did you kill them?" Crow asks Liam.

"No, Gray stopped me. Said Char might want to get her own revenge one day. The rest of them have probably scattered by now, but those two are at the club in one of the interrogation rooms." This is news to me as much as it seems to be to Crow.

"They are?" I ask, wondering for the first time if revenge would help. I feel OK most of the time. Like genuinely ok, but then there are other times when I look at the scars littering my body and all I want to do is sob and sit in a bath of bleach to rid my body of the invisible dirt and grime that only I can see.

Liam nods next to me but doesn't say anything else.

It doesn't take me long to imagine a scenario in which I could harm them. I know I'm not the first person they've nearly killed. They've killed and damaged many women before me from what Gray told me, but does that mean they deserve what my imagination could conjure? Yeah, actually, they do deserve it.

"If I wanted that, you'd help me?" I ask them both.

"I'd love to fucking kill them myself, but if seeing you do it is my only option, then I'll bring the damn popcorn," Crow says as his hand grazes mine.

"I nearly killed them once already, I'm not opposed to helping you finish the job," Liam confirms.

Knowing that they're both so willing to lay down themselves to help me makes me feel more powerful than I should. I remember wondering if part of the reason that Liam is attracted to me is because of the power role he had over me - being older, more experienced, and having lived and experienced more, but I realise now that the truth with both of them is that I'm the one in charge. I'm the one with the power, and I like that thought more than I assumed I would.

I decide to be brave, if that's even the right word, as I ask them, "Would you kneel for me?"

Crow and Liam both have near identical confusion flitting across their faces before they both nod as they look me up and down.

"Then kneel."

I watch as hunger begins to fill their gazes, their minds obviously realising how this could end up. I want to test it. I want to see how it feels. I've always submitted, even when fighting, I've always been the one to submit and for the first time in my life, I want to be the one in charge. Of everything.

One by one, Liam slightly more hesitant than Crow, they kneel on the floor in front of me. I know no one's going to walk in. Crow locked the door behind us when we came into the gym earlier, not wanting anyone to interrupt me while training.

I inch closer to them, their heads directly opposite my upper stomach. I'm only around a foot away from them now, and I find my insides pooling with a heat I didn't expect. The sight of them submissively knelt beneath me has me feeling more in control and powerful than I ever have. I feel like a queen sitting on a throne with someone worshipping me. Only in my case, I get two someones.

"Lay down," I instruct them. They do exactly as I say within seconds, their speed almost comical as I watch them.

"Closer. I want your sides touching." They don't say a word but shift closer together. Crow has a smirk on his face while Liam looks more tentative and confused.

I walk towards them and take a seat on Liam's hips, feeling his cock lengthen beneath my core instantly as I smile down at him, my face no doubt coating with desire as I grind my body along him. He lets out a low moan as his eyes roll back and his hands grapple to find my waist.

I look to Crow and find him still smiling deviously, his head lifting and finding mine, our lips connecting as I continue the movement over Liam.

The moment Crows lips find mine, Liam begins thrusting up into me. Even with our clothes in the way, the warmth filling me is undeniable. The multi-layered pleasure has me bucking and reaching for Crow's dick with my hand, allowing Liam's hands on my waist and Crow's hand wrapped around my head to hold me up.

"I could fucking eat you, princess. Fuck, I've missed you," Crow grunts out as he pulls my head towards his, his tongue fighting with mine for dominance as Liam's hand pulls my head back by my hair. My eyes catch his. The pleasure and hunger in his eyes as he watches Crow and I ignites the burning desire within me even further.

"Open the [BH1] fucking door! We got a problem!" I hadn't heard anything before that, but the abrupt voice pulls me out of my daze as I pull away from Liam and Crow. I stand immediately with the worry of someone barging in through the locked door.

"Fuck me, he had to come now?" Crow groans as he stands and adjusts himself, followed by Liam who does the same before going to the door and opening it to find my dad there. He's glaring at Liam until his eyes find mine. I have no doubt that my skin is as blushed as I feel and my hair as messy as my heart as he rolls his eyes at me and instructs us to follow him.

Nineteen

CHARLIE

The problem was not in fact a problem but rather us being too obvious. Oops.

We've been going at this fighting malarkey for days, which I understand isn't really much, but it feels like years and in that time, the only thing I've mastered is hiding, avoiding being punched, and tiring someone out--which was exactly the goal so that sounds great but today, Crow said he was going to put in real effort. I thought I was ready, more than ready. I was not ready. It took me three attempts before I managed to avoid getting hit. He wasn't hitting me hard at all, just little jabs, but he was using his full speed and skill as my opponent will and I failed epically. The problem with this is that I don't have long left and whereas Crow was taking it lightly on me, I know that Theo will not give me the courtesy of trying again or going easy on me.

"As long as you can wear him out and avoid him grabbing or hitting you, you'll be fine. Wait until he's tired and then put your all into it. Get him on the floor. You want to go for his head, try and twist or break some bones if you can. If he's weak, he'll give in easier or the ref will call it," Liam tells me. I've heard this so many times and yet the closer we get to the match, the more terrified I become of getting into a ring with someone that is nearly twice my size. Someone that is going to put everything he has into beating me up.

"Why did I sign up for this again?" I ask with a defeated laugh as I slump down on the kitchen chair.

"Because you're a badass bitch with the Irish Mafia, The Cobras, and The Devils Dealers supporting you. Maybe," Crow tells me with a smirk and a light knock to the shoulder as I wince.

"Don't touch me. Everything hurts." I moan as I close my eyes and lay my head down on the table in front of me.

"What are you thinking about tomorrow?" Liam asks as he retrieves the ice from the freezer and fills up a glass of juice for me.

Tomorrow. Oh, shit, I had practically forgotten all about tomorrow. My dad had arranged for David, my biological father (that sounds too weird), to come and meet me. He is coming here, to my dad's house, which helps the anxiety but that doesn't make me any less nervous to meet some random man.

"I'm thinking that I have way too much going on in my life right now already, but I know that if I put off meeting him then it'll just make it harder," I tell them honestly.

I've been so busy during the previous days that I hadn't had time to think about tomorrow and how I expected or wished it would go, but that doesn't change the fact that now that I am thinking about it my stomach is tensing and my mind is racing in the worst possible way.

"Do you know him?" I ask Liam. He was around when my mum was, so maybe he does. Maybe he can tell me something to calm my nerves.

"Not personally. Your dad said I met him years ago, but I don't remember it. We've done plenty of looking him up so that we know he's a decent guy but honestly, that's about it. I'm sorry, baby," he says as he runs his hand through my hair.

"It's alright. It's life. It'll be fine. Everything is always fine eventually," I tell him with a weak smile.

I'm not nervous. Yet. Although I'm sure I will be come morning.

"You two will stay here, won't you?"

"We'll always stay, I told you I'm never leaving you again and I damn well meant it," Crow tells me with conviction as Liam nods in agreement.

"Who damn well meant what?" Gray asks as he waltzes into the kitchen.

"You look a mess, Chars, what the hell did you do?" he asks as he looks me up and down, horror written all over his face, before he goes to the fridge and gets his overnight oats out. He's obsessed. Has them every morning without fail.

"I damn well meant that I ain't leaving her," Crow repeats.

"Oh yeah, he won't even come to the bloody Club with me. He's besotted," Gray comments casually as he sits beside me and begins eating.

"You would be, too, if you let yourself open up to a certain someone," Crow tells him with a look that says 'mhmm, I know'.

"You need to stop gossiping with the Cobras like a bunch of old fucking ladies is what you need to do. You're meant to be my best friend," Gray says with a mouthful of food as he points at Crow and then to himself as he speaks.

"I am, but since you won't listen, I'm just reiterating my point that you're a fucking idiot that'll end up alone unless you let someone in."

"Someone isn't who I want, I don't know who I want otherwise I would," Gray utters.

"Are you not even gonna stick up for me here? We went through legitimate trauma together and you're letting him rip into me?" Gray asks Liam, his face an image of shock.

"If I didn't agree with him, I'd totally take his side but as it happens, he's right for once," Liam says as he continues roaming his hands through my hair, totally unbothered by anyone around us.

"You guys are shit today, I am so not keen on you two right now. So much for being my fucking bestie beans. What time's your maker coming tomorrow?" Gray asks me as he changes the subject.

Crow covers his mouth as he attempts to hide a laugh - failing epically too, might I add. I give him a short glare before turning my attention back to Gray.

"He is not my maker," I hiss out, "and I don't know, I'm pretty sure Dad told me but I've forgotten. Are you sticking around tomorrow too?" I wonder.

"Are you kidding me? I love you, but hell no. It's weird enough knowing our mother's a hoe that kept half your DNA hidden, but I do not need to meet that half. What if I find him really attractive and end up screwing your daddy? Oh, that would be a good story. You should write that. Take notes." He hands me my phone and waves his hand around in a writing motion as if to tell me to get on with it.

"You are so disturbed," I huff out with a laugh that follows as I take my phone from him.

"For being gay or for potentially being into your daddy?" he asks, his eyebrows wagging my way with a smirk.

Even though I've suspected as much many times, this is the first time Gray has ever openly told me that he's gay, and the fact that he's doing it in such a relaxed way makes me beyond happy. I worried for such a long time that he felt the pressure of making an announcement when I don't think it should ever be that way. It should be as simple as saying, 'hey, I love this person'.

"Definitely the second option." I laugh, enjoying the glee on Gray's face.

"What type of guy would you go for? I mean, if I ever potentially found someone that I thought would be a good fit for you?" I wonder.

"Are you kidding me? Isn't it obvious?" Crow asks, his head falling back with a laugh as he pats a glaring Gray on the shoulder.

"What? No, why would it be obvious?"

"He's a little baby bottom, aren't you, bro?" Crow says as he ruffles Gray's hair.

"I honestly don't know why we're friends at this point," Gray mutters grumpily.

"I thought you were fucking Ben?" Liam asks, his eyes wide as if trying to figure out how that worked since Ben gave off major bottom energy.

I'd been curious about their flirtatious nature for a while but didn't want to intrude by asking.

"Haven't found anyone worth being a bottom for." He shrugs.

"Wait, so are you and Ben actually a thing?" I ask.

Liam nods his head at me and gets a glare from Gray.

"No, we are not a thing. We just mess around sometimes. He's too... nice," he says with a grimace just as Dad walks in behind him.

"Who's too nice?"

All of our eyes divert to my dad, Gray's wide eyes included.

"Liam," I say, completely unsure of why, but it was the first name that came into my head.

My dad's brows crease. "Liam's too nice?" he asks, his voice totally unbelieving. "For what? A fucking mass murderer? That's about the only thing he won't do." He huffs and rolls his eyes and pulls his phone out of his pocket.

"How's the fighting going? Victor said Theo's in impeccable shape," he tells us, showing us a clip on his phone of Theo sparring with someone.

"Victor sent you that? He's a fucking shithead, I don't care how much sucking up he does," Crow says, shaking his head and leaning back from the phone screen so that I can see.

"Yep, he's been keeping me in the loop," my dad tells us.

I watch the video, my face practically glued to the screen as I witness the brutal punches and lethal force that leaves Theo as he trains with a man I don't know or recognise. The strength and power behind his punches terrifies me. The idea of him coming towards me with that force sends shivers down my spine, makes my hands shake, and my heart race far more quickly than should be possible.

"I'm not trying to put you down here, darlin', but I'd prefer the club go to him by you forfeiting than see you get hurt in the process of trying to win it." I understand why he's worried. I'm worried and I'd be surprised if he wasn't. He's seen Gray and I go through so much pain that I can understand why he doesn't want to witness anymore of it, but despite how much Theo terrifies me, I know that I can't give up now. I know that I have to at least try.

"I'm not giving up to that," I say, my head nodding to the screen still held out towards us in his hand.

"I'm not letting the likes of him run the Cobras into the ground after years of them having us. They have us or they have nothing. He's not winning anything other than a trip to hospital," I tell them all with far more confidence than I actually have.

I remember my dad telling us that confidence is all you need. He said you could scare people with confidence. So long as they thought you could beat them, then you could. I've never put that theory to the test but now is as good a time as any, right?

Twenty

CHARLIE

"Will you stop fidgeting, darlin', it'll be fine," my dad says as he gets his rucksack together for work. I untangle my hands and place them on my lap.

I'm meeting David today. He's driven two hours to meet me for the first time, and it's only because I don't want to be rude and disrespectful to the effort that he's gone through that I don't bolt out the back door right now.

"I know."

"What is it about meeting him that makes you so nervous?" he asks.

I ponder his question, not completely sure of the answer. In less than five minutes, David will be here. I can't decipher what I'm thinking, let alone put it into words. I don't really know why I'm nervous, other than knowing that this meeting could go wrong, feel weird, or be a lot more tense than I'd like.

I've had different scenarios running through my head all night and every moment of the day since I woke up. This could go terribly. He might see me, see the scar on my face that I've done my very best to forget about, and wonder what happened, as any normal human being would. I don't want to lie to the man the very first time I meet him, but there's also no chance of me telling him the truth. He might meet me, begin talking to me, and decide that I'm a terrible person that he doesn't want to get to know, and it's not as though I particularly want to impress him or anything, but it would be nice for him to meet me and think that I'm not a bad person. I don't ever try to be. I try to be the opposite, although I admittedly don't always succeed in that.

"I don't know. It's just a weird situation. I'm just stressing," I state.

"That it is," he says with a chuckle.

The doorbell goes, and I'm sure I'm about to pee my pants as Dad gives me a warm smile before heading to open it. I follow behind him. He's acting so chilled out, though I'm willing to bet at least some of that is for my sake because he can see that I'm nervous.

He opens the door and I'm presented with a man that if I wasn't sure before that he was my biological father, then I am now.

I instantly see it, the resemblance between us. He has the same shade of grassy green eyes as I do, the same freckles under his slightly wrinkled skin. He's older than Dad is, that much is obvious, though not by more than ten years I'd say.

I smile weakly at him and see an identical one trained back onto me. We have the same smile. It's like looking into a mirror if I take away the fact that he's however many years older than me and a man.

Ok, maybe not a very good mirror, maybe a blurry mirror or the strange ones you get at amusement parks for kids.

He's wearing dark jeans and a white long-sleeved shirt. He looks smart, posh almost. He has no stubble, no beard or moustache, and has hair the same dull brown colour as mine cut neatly atop his head.

"Come on in. You can sit in the kitchen with Charl, I was

just heading out," Dad says as he leads us back through to the kitchen.

I take a seat in the same spot I was before, easing myself into the comfortable worn wooden chair as David does the same in the seat opposite me after Dad gives him the nod of encouragement to sit.

"I can see the resemblance between us already, you look just like my daughter," David states as he smiles warmly at me.

"You've got a daughter?" The question I was about to blurt out comes out of Dad's mouth instead. I like that he is just as curious as I am.

"Yes. Yes." He smiles. "She's just a few years older than you. I have a son as well."

"Will you tell me about them?" I ask enthusiastically.

"You know what, I'm gonna head off to work, I'll leave you two be. Liam and Crow are in the living room if you need them," he reassures me with a small smile.

He walks over to me and gives me a kiss on the top of my head before saying a swift "love you" and running off.

"You can see that you two love each other a lot," David says with what looks to be a genuine smile.

"I don't mean to offend you when I say this but he's my dad. It would probably be stranger if we didn't love each other."

He smiles knowingly at me.

"No, I completely understand. I do want you to know, though, that I do love you as well. Since the moment your dad rang me and told me everything, I've loved you and it's only grown more and more every day." I feel so cruel not being able to return the kind sentiment, but I'm hoping he understands that for me it's just too soon, something that isn't yet there or formed. I'd only be lying if I repeated his words back to him.

"So, you were going to tell me about your kids?" I encourage.

"Ah, yes!" he exclaims.

He leans down to the bag I didn't notice before and pulls out what looks to be a scrapbook.

"I know it's a little childish, but we've all been creating little notes and pictures for you since we found out." He hands me the book and nods at me to open it.

I open the first page and find a picture of David, with who I assume to be his son, daughter, and wife.

His wife has beautiful fiery, short red hair, warm grey eyes, and a large smile. She looks like the mums you see in movies, the ones that want to constantly make sure you're fed, hydrated, and hugged just enough.

The girl in the picture does look surprisingly similar to me. She has her dad's dark hair that falls just above her shoulders. She has a button nose like I do, with grey eyes like her mother. Our face shapes are very similar, but her skin is lighter than mine.

The young man in the picture had the same warm smile as his mum; stood next to his sister with his arm around her shoulders. He's looking directly at the camera. He has auburn hair, a mixture of both his mother and father's, though he has the same green eyes as I do. The shape of his eyes is similar to mine as well. His smile is infectious, even through the picture.

I look down at the names below the picture. David. His wife Amanda, Robin, and Dustin.

I turn the page quickly and find a handwritten letter attached to the page alongside a bookmark.

"I'm not really sure how I'm supposed to start this letter, but I wanted to write something to you, so I'm going to start again.

Dear Charlie, (that seems a little too formal, doesn't it?)
To my new sister (that seems too cringey)
Hey! (I'm giving up with the greeting now, so stopping here)"

I find myself laughing at the letter before carrying on.

"Considering I'm a writer for a living, I'm really not doing very well here.

Dad's told me a bit about you, but I don't think he knows loads yet, so I'm still a little clueless.

He says you like books, so I've given you one of my bookmarks. I love to read too, I'm actually a professional writer so if you ever fancy turning reading or writing into a career then hit me up!

I already have one little sister but because of how old we are I didn't think I'd ever get another. Mum and Dad definitely aren't going to be starting all over again with a baby anytime soon. So, when he told us about you, I've got to admit that I nearly had a legitimate heart attack. I mean, not exactly but I full on thought I was going to. He came into the lounge calling a family meeting one night and came out with that! He says you only just found out, too, and I'm sorry for that. We're all excited to meet you, but I get that for you it's probably more stressful than exciting.

I really can't wait to see you.

I'm not really sure what I'm supposed to be saying in this letter. I'm just rambling at the moment, as I'm sure you can tell. But I just wanted you to know that I'm happy that you're going to be a part of our family, I'm happy that I've got another little sister. With any luck you won't be as annoying as my other one. But overall, I can't wait to meet you.

From the best big brother that you'll ever have (yes, I hear you have a brother but I'm competitive. I'll win.)

Dustin

P.S Can we meet you soon?"

I find myself laughing again at his all over the place letter, but I do appreciate it all the same.

"Dustin seems keen to meet me," I say with a laugh.

"I had to fight him off coming with me today, he's persistent alright," David tells me with a smile.

"What's he like?" I ask.

He takes a moment, searching off in space as he conducts his words.

"He's thoughtful, caring beyond measure, and a complete nuisance too, though he'd disagree with me about that." His soft smile looks so honest that I can't help but trust the words he's telling me.

"I take it he didn't convince you to let him come then?"

David physically cringes at my words, and I watch as he pulls his eyebrows together. What's that about?

"I didn't want to tell you in case you felt pressured, but I don't want to lie to you since you've asked. He's in the car. He said he wanted to come even if he just got to see your face from the door," he tells me hesitantly.

I find myself laughing again.

"Can I go get him?" I ask, curious to meet the grown man that is sitting in the car alone just to get a five-second sighting of me. I suddenly feel like a statue in a museum. It makes me feel like a celebrity with paparazzi on my tail. I smile at the thought.

"You really don't have to if you don't want to. He knew there was a chance he wouldn't meet you. You don't have to meet him just because he came here," he rushes out. I like more than I'll admit how diligent David is in making me feel comfortable.

"It's ok, it would be nice to meet him," I admit.

David looks up at me warily, obviously unsure of my words.

"Plus, he's probably less likely to annoy you for two hours with questions on the way home if I meet him," I say with what I hope to be a convincing smile.

"As long as you're sure," he tells me with a weak smile.

I nod and enter the hallway towards the door, walking past the mirror and stopping abruptly. Because I'm so used to it now, I forget the scar is there, but I realise that David hasn't looked at it once, nor asked about it and although I'm surprised by that, it pleases me to no end. I wonder if his son will have the same reaction, or lack of, as his dad or if he'll be curious enough to ask.

I walk out the front door and find the man from the picture leaning against what I assume to be David's car, looking down at a book in his hands. He's not noticed me yet.

"Dustin?" I ask.

He looks up instantly and a wary smile fills his face.

"Are you Charlie?" he asks hesitantly. He closes his book and takes a step towards me.

"Shit, you look just like Robin, you must be you." I laugh at his logic.

"Are you coming inside?"

"Seriously? You don't mind?" I don't ask, but by his appearance I'd say he's probably early twenties, but the way his voice lifts with excitement, he seems like a little kid.

"Yeah, come on." I usher him inside behind me and lead him into the kitchen. He takes a seat next to David.

"Do either of you want a cuppa? I forgot to ask when you came in, sorry, David," I say as I begin boiling the kettle.

"Tea would be fantastic, please, Charlie. We both take one sugar," David tells me.

I make the tea quickly and hand it to them before taking a seat back at the table.

"You're really pretty." I blush at Dustin's abrupt compliment, not used to being told that by anyone other than Liam, Crow, and my dad occasionally.

"Thank you," I tell him with an awkward laugh.

"It seems weird hearing you call Dad David. I know you've got your own dad, but it still seems strange," he says with a chuckle.

"Yeah, I suppose I'd think it was weird too if I was in your situation," I say with a smile.

"My sister's going to hate how pretty you are," he says with a boisterous laugh.

My eyes go wide as I look at David.

"Have you not seen the scar on my face? She's got nothing to worry about." I laugh.

The idea of her hating me instils a panic inside of me that I didn't expect. I don't plan on becoming besties with them all, but I didn't want her to hate me.

"How'd you get it?" Dustin asks causally as he takes a sip of his tea.

"Dustin, stop it. You're making her feel awkward," David admonishes. Although he's right, I don't like the idea that Dustin feels bad for trying to get to know me.

"No, it's ok. Everyone's naturally curious about things like that, I get it. I would be too if one of you walked in with a scar covering half your face," I say with a tender smile.

"I was attacked not so long ago, the same day as I had the swabs for the DNA sample actually, not as though my dad told me this is what they were for. I ended up in hospital and am now covered in all these wonderful scars that I should totally make up stories about to make me sound like a badass," I say with a laugh.

David and Dustin look at each other briefly before turning back to me.

"Did your dad sort the people out that attacked you?" David asks warily.

I realise that he didn't ask if the police had. That makes me curious. Does he know about the Club? Liam said he knew David when he was around years ago, so I suppose he would, but would I jeopardise them by saying yes, they did? I don't actually know the answer.

"I don't know, I haven't asked to be honest with you. Do you... do you know what Dad does?" I wonder.

David smiles at me. "Yes. I'm well aware of what your father does for a living. I have no issue at all with your father or the lifestyle he lives," he says to me reassuringly.

"That's great and all, but are either of you going to tell me?"

Dustin asks, and I can't help but smile at his impatience at being left out.

"Charlie's father owns a Club. A Club that's," he pauses for a moment, "that's not completely legal in all of their actions," he tells Dustin.

I smile at his evaluation of it. He's not wrong by any means, but he's put it so delicately that it almost makes it sound ok, when I know that the majority of society don't think it is.

"And you haven't intercepted yet?" My ears perk at this. Intercepted? My narrow eyes find their way towards David.

"Why would you intercept the Club? How?" I ask, my tone making my thoughts clear.

David shuffles uncomfortably before he puts his hand in the breast pocket of his jacket and brings out the one thing every one of us dread.

Detective.

"Get out." I stand as I say the words, pulling the gun from its hidden spot under the table as I do, thankful that I remember years after my dad told me about hidden guns around the house. Pointing it directly at David's head, I wait patiently for them to leave. I've been through far too much shit to even contemplate letting a man like this worm his way in. He's probably just using me to get to the Club.

"Get out or I will kill you right now," I say when David doesn't make a move to go.

He's using his connection to me to get in. He's using it to arrest and hurt the Club and the family I've always loved. I will not allow him to hurt them. I couldn't care less about who he is.

Dustin's eyes bug so far out that if I wasn't so pissed I'd probably have laughed at his cartoon-like face.

"Woah, woah, it's ok." He has his hands up in front of him as he stands, towering above me.

"Get out. Now." I try to keep my voice as low and steady as I can.

Liam and Crow barge in, their eyes flicking to me for only a second before they get their own guns out and point them at David.

Crow turns to me, asking, "Sorry to break the tension here, but why are we holding him at gunpoint, princess?"

"He's a detective," I tell him coolly.

"That's why you have a gun pointed at him?" Liam asks as he brings his arm down and places the gun back into the behind of his jeans. Why is he putting it away, the bloody idiot?

"I'm not here to take anything down. I've known about the Club for years. I have no issue with your father running it, none at all," he says.

"What the actual fuck is happening?" Dustin asks more to himself, I think, than anyone else as he watches the shitshow commence. I pay him no mind.

"He's not going to do anything to put anyone away or put the Club at jeopardy, Char, do you really think your dad and I would have let him in if we thought he was?" Liam asks.

"You knew he was a detective?" I ask incredulously, pointing my narrowed eyes at Liam this time.

"Well yeah, but he's not bad, baby," he tells me.

I realise he's right. Dad and Liam would have done every possible check they needed to before letting him in, especially with all the crap going on at the moment.

I bring my arm down, the gun alongside it, and watch as Crow does the same, following my lead.

"Fine. I don't give a shit who you are though, you hurt my family and I will kill you and make sure no one ever finds you." I know I shouldn't threaten people, especially this guy. My biological father. Especially a detective that I don't actually have a way of getting rid of or plan on shooting. My plan is just to scare him which apparently now makes me look like an idiot.

"I don't doubt that one bit," he tells me steadily.

"Sit down and drink your damn tea," I tell him with a sigh and a roll of my eyes at my own ridiculous jump from A to Z.

"I'm sorry for threatening to shoot you. Probably not the best first impression," I say as I smile and shift uncomfortably.

He chuckles as he looks at me. "One of the best first impressions I've ever experienced actually."

"You're a fucking badass bitch!" Dustin exclaims excitedly. I roll my eyes again and laugh at his absurdity.

"That is definitely not something I've ever been called before," I lie as my eyes meet Crow's, holding back the laughter that threatens to spill.

"That was insanely cool!" he says to me, before turning to his father. "Why didn't you teach us to do shit like that?" he asks.

I laugh at him and take my previous seat.

"You may as well stay now that you're here," I tell Crow and Liam.

"Dustin, David, this is Liam," I say, nodding to Liam. "And Crow," I say, smiling up at Crow.

They all nod at each other in greeting.

"You literally live in a film. That was so cool. You've just given me the best idea for a new book," David says as he shakes his head in astonishment.

Twenty-One

CHARLIE

"I feel like I'm literally going to shit myself," I announce to Liam and Crow as they start putting the weights back on the shelves in front of me. We have the gym to ourselves again. My last training session is over, and now the fight that could change everything is mere hours away.

An abrupt laugh leaves both Crow and Liam.

"OK, don't do that, not only would it be extremely unattractive-" Crow starts.

"I don't aim to be attractive," I interrupt.

"And that's not where I was going with this if you'd let me finish my sentence, little miss stress head. I was going to say, not only would that be extremely unattractive but it would also put you in a bad mood for tonight which is not what you want. You want to be in a good mood," he finishes as he comes closer to me and lifts my lips into a smile with his fingers.

"No, a bad mood would mean she was more lethal. Do it. Shit yourself," Liam says from across the room as a laugh escapes me at his stern expression and simple order of encouragement.

"I vote no," Crow says with a look of confusion in Liam's direction.

"Do you think it'll help if I puke? Maybe I just need to be sick," I think out loud, nodding my head as if answering my own question.

"I vote no for that too. But I'm sure Liam would love to disagree with me and suggest that you simultaneously shit yourself and puke. Shall we add piss in, too, Liam? You into that?" Crow asks before turning to me again, "Go for it. Shit, piss, and puke on yourself, it'll help," he says mockingly in a tone that I assume is meant to be Liam's.

Liam knocks his shoulder, "I do not sound like that and no, I'm not suggesting she let every bodily fluid suddenly hammer out of her. I'm just saying that her being in a happy go lucky mood isn't going to help her win a fight," Liam says, pinching the bridge of his nose as he looks between me and Crow.

"OK, you two are ridiculous and not helping at all." I laugh, watching as the two men smirk at one another.

Fuck, my body sees them and within seconds just wants to pounce.

So not the time, Charlie.

"What do we do now? I feel like I need to stay busy or I'll get nervous, and I don't want to be nervous." My goal is to appear as confident as possible even if that's not actually how I feel.

"I can think of plenty of things to keep you busy," Crow says with a dramatic wag of his brows and a wink in my direction.

"Even when being ridiculous, you are ridiculously handsome. Flop it on out and I'm all for it," I joke with a shrug.

"No, that is not going to help. Not right now at least," Liam intercedes, rolling his eyes once more.

"I mean, it might help me relieve some pressure."

"Then let us relieve your pressure, not the other way around," Liam says as he stalks towards me and takes my face in his hands, his lips crashing into mine in a show of dominance and passion that I am all for.

He arches my head backwards, so that my face is directly below his as he devours my mouth with his own, his tongue darting between our lips as I feel Crow's presence behind me, his lips on my neck and his hands between my legs.

"Knock, knock, I'm coming in!" a voice shouts from outside the door.

Oh, for fuck's sake, not again.

Crow groans behind me as he steps away, Liam simultaneously pulling his lips from mine as he lets out a sigh of frustration, his pants tenting without care as Gray walks in.

"I feel like I just interrupted something," Gray says as he takes in our positions. Crow is mere inches from me at my back while Liam still has his hand around the back of my head.

"You did. You can go now and come back later," Liam says as he walks towards Gray and begins ushering him out.

"Uhrm, no actually, I can't. I need advice. Like, now," he says as he skirts around Liam and comes barrelling towards me in a rush, as if worried that Liam will catch him and physically toss him out.

"What's up?" I ask as I take a seat on the gym benches and gesture for Gray to do the same on the ones in front of me.

"I think Ben likes me," he blurts out, cringing as if it's the worst thing in the world.

"Why do you think he likes you?" I'm not even sure why I'm asking this question considering the way that Ben looks at him. Every time they're in the same room, Gray is completely unfased and Ben acts like a man starved for the sight of my brother.

"Because he told me he likes me."

"So you know that he likes you?" I ask.

"Well, he could have just been saying it."

"Why would he do that?"

I'm sure my face conveys the confusion I'm feeling because he quickly starts talking again.

"I mean, I know he's attracted to me, we've been fucking on

and off for ages, but he said he likes me," he emphasises as if this makes more sense than his previous statement.

"Is that a bad thing?" I wonder, unsure of why this is such a problem.

"Well, yeah, that's why I'm seeking advice, Chars. Duh." He rolls his eyes, watching me as if I've completely lost my mind, which I may very well have considering I don't understand what the issue is.

"Oh, I get it, you don't like him, you just want to fuck him," Crow says with a nod of understanding.

"Exactly."

"So, what is it you need advice on? How to make him not like you? Just be yourself. I don't like you," Liam states - a complete lie if I've ever heard one.

"You only don't like me because I interrupted your weird time with my sister and Crow, which might I add for a second time is weird," Gray acknowledges.

"You told me when I was like ten that you would never judge me. This feels pretty judgey," I argue.

"No, no, no, I'm judging him," he says with a look in Liam's begruntled direction, "and him," he says as he nods towards Crow, "but I'm not judging you." he clarifies.

Despite his reassurance, I somehow don't think the words coming out of his mouth are making the situation any better.

"That's judging, mate," Crow tells him.

"OK, well fine, I'm judging. Now back to the problem at hand please. What do I do?"

"Be honest with him. Tell him that you don't see him that way and that you're not going to carry on having sex because you don't want to lead him on," I tell him, not understanding how this is even a question he needs to ask.

Is it not common sense to do the above? I mean, obviously not if Gray seems to be having so much difficulty coming to the same conclusion that I have.

"Yeah, but I get stressed if I don't have sex for too long."

"Have sex with someone else then, it's not hard, mate."

"It is when there's fuck all gay people around. I don't mess with baby bi's, and I literally don't know any other gay person," he concludes.

"Aren't there apps for shit like that?" Liam asks as he grabs Crow's phone from out of his hand and begins looking up gay hookup apps and showing Gray.

"Yes, but I'm a depresso espresso that doesn't want to just meet random people for sex. Who knows what they'll do to me? I don't want to be kidnapped and raped, thank you very much. Not my kink," he says as he lifts his hands in the air and shakes his head.

His eyes catch mine at the exact moment he realises what he's said.

"OK, that was bad. I should not have said that. I'm sorry, I didn't think. Too soon, always gonna be too soon," he hashes out in a panicked rush as he waits for a reaction from me.

"It's fine." I smile, knowing he meant no harm and that he just doesn't have a filter between his brain and his mouth. "I get what you mean and from experience, I can vouch that you do not want that. Been there, done that, got the t-shirt," I say as I pull the shirt I'm wearing in front of me as if to show him.

"You realise how weird you two are, right?" Crow asks as he looks between Gray and I with confusion marring his brows.

"Yeah, we're odd, get over it. You love us both; now hush while my sister gives me some solid advice," Gray tells him with a pat on his shoulder and a hand on his mouth to silence him.

"Ew, don't lick me, you freak! Jesus, keep your animals under control, Charlie," Gray says as he pulls his hand back from Crow, wipes his palm on his trousers, and watches him in disgust as an obnoxious laugh leaves me, Crow, and Liam at Gray's reaction.

"OK, OK, my advice is to find someone else to hook up with, be honest with Ben, and be chill. Meet in public places, tell people where you're going, and do that thing where you check peoples' criminal records."

"Ugh, you just don't understand." He groans as he gets up to leave, "Oh, and Dad wants to see you." He checks the time on his phone and holds it up for us to see. "Like twenty minutes ago."

∼

"Are you ready?"

No.

"Yep," I lie, watching as my dad paces nervously around the room.

I'm nervous, I'm anxious and I'm scared, but the nervous energy emitting from my father is absolutely killing me and making me so much worse.

"Stop pacing, she can't stop watching you," Liam tells my dad, his eyes not leaving mine as he speaks. He's been doing this all day. Watching me as if waiting for me to break down. I mean, I very well might so it's not a bad idea for him to keep an eye on me.

"Hey, princess!" Crow shouts from across the room as he jogs over to me.

"What?" I ask, not wanting to let too many words come out for the worry that I may very well just tell them all that I'm giving up and not doing this anymore.

"The crowd's filling out, Theo's looking like a bitch boy in his spandex, and you're about to become the president of the mother fucking Dark Cobras. You ready for this shit? My princess is about to get queen status people, it's time to move your butts!" he yells at the people milling around us as the few people in here smile, nod, or shout a cheer in our direction.

We're currently in the gym - again with Tin, my dad (Matt), Alice, David, Gray (who said he did indeed find David attractive - great), Liam, and Crow.

"I'm not doing nothing, I'm just waiting," My dad responds to Liam.

"You're about to boss the fuck out of this shit and if for any reason you want to give up, just give me or Liam a shout and we'll come save your ass, k?"

So not ok.

"OK." I nod. I attempt to drown out the chatter and noise from around me with my music but every time I put the headphones in, someone comes up to me to say something and I zone out again.

"It's time to go, baby girl," Liam whispers to me, his face so close that I can feel his breath on my lips.

"OK."

Be cool. Be calm. Be confident.

Twenty-Two

VICTOR

Even though it's one of my father's men fighting, I'm not sure how welcome I'll be to attend considering the way things panned out between me and Charlie.

I hold no ill will towards her, despite what I can understand those that care about her believe and by some miracle, she doesn't seem to have any hatred for me.

She saunters in, the complete image of someone cool and collected, gives me a hug, asks me to secretly spike Theo, tells me she is joking, laughs, and off she goes. So simple. Elegant. Confident. I highly doubt she is truly feeling that way, but the air of it is the perfect persona for this evening's events.

I've already drugged him, unbeknownst to her. I'm not going to tell her that - or anyone for that matter. I needed to do something in an attempt to gain the forgiveness she has already granted me, after all. I had no illusions of what I was doing. I know I need to do much, much more to truly attempt to gain her trust, but this is a start even if she will never be made aware of it.

I watch from the bar as the area fills with people. I know most of them or, if I don't know them personally, I recognise or have heard of them at least. It's how it often works in this world.

You may not know someone, but you always know of them. Usually because of some story that has been told with dramatic changes to enhance the truth of the situation.

"Can I get you another, sweetie?" the bartender, Ben I believe his name was, asks.

I shake my head, but notice that his eyes aren't on me as he speaks, they are across the room. Out of curiosity, I allow my eyes to follow his line of sight. Gray. Ben is looking at him with an intensity and hunger I recognise. I wonder to myself if it is a one-sided crush or if Gray swings that way. I don't recall Charlie ever mentioning it, but perhaps she doesn't know. Or perhaps I've got it all wrong. Or perhaps it is simply not an advertised fact.

My mind takes me to unimaginable places as I witness made up images of Gray bending Ben over and pounding into him. The thought of it has me feeling more uncomfortable and hotter than I'd like. I haven't ever envisioned a man in a sexual way before, but the images keep coming and coming. I attempt to distract myself by looking around the room and taking in my surroundings but nothing does the trick, the images won't leave me. They are all I can see.

Gray on his knees.

Gray on his stomach, arse up.

Gray begging, pleading, screaming.

Fuck, I can imagine absolutely ruining him. I can imagine his hair soaked with sweat and cum as he looks up at me.

Shake out of it, for fuck's sake.

I have no idea where or why the pictures of him naked for me are appearing, but they won't stop. I have absolutely no problem with anyone's sexuality but mine has always been very simply straight - until I noticed Ben watching him with desire, that is.

I'd only met him the once at Charlie's father's home when I explained myself to her. I wince just thinking about that day - not because of the physical pain caused - I'd had much worse but rather because of the devastation it had caused Charlie and the trust that we had grown that had been so irrevocably shattered.

It wasn't as simple as I'd made it out to be, but without jeopardising the person I care for most in the world, I couldn't very well go and explain that to anyone, could I? No, I need to protect them from anyone that could know of their existence and if that means taking the consequences of actions I wish I didn't have to take in the first place, then so be it. I am surprised that they believed that I'd taken action based off of threats towards my father considering how little love there was between us, but they did believe it and that's all that matters. I don't need questions asked that I don't wish to answer.

I realise that through the process of my thoughts wandering astray that I must still have been looking at Gray, who was now looking at me with eyes filled with hatred. Great. One more person to add to the list.

I can't help but notice how attractive he is. He has a rather boyish look about him that seems to appeal to me. I'm sure Charlie mentioned that he was a few years older than her, possibly around twenty-one, but he looks like the type of man that could be fifty and look half his age. He has an innocent look about him that I know holds no fact. He is far from an innocent person. Not a bad one that I am aware of, but certainly not innocent either.

His attire replicates that of a teenager in college with his grey tracksuit bottoms that get tighter towards his ankles and a dark hoodie that looks to be far too big on him. He has a slender body. He is built with muscle from what I saw the other day, but more of a swimmer's fitness level than that of a fighter with hordes of muscle. Sandy blonde hair covers his head and sweeps lightly across his forehead. I'd noticed him moving his fringe out of the way the day at their father's but hadn't taken much notice of anything else about him. He's a few inches shorter than me, though given how tall I am, that's not a surprise.

Stop staring, Victor.

Right, right. I'm here for Charlie.

I turn my attention back to the self-made ring in the centre of the room and watch as Crow, Liam, Tin, and Matt gear Charlie up. She looks surprisingly level headed considering the jibes and curses coming her way from Theo across the ring. He's doing his very best to antagonise her, I can see it in his eyes. He's wearing an evil smirk that I've seen many times before. He's a big man. Maybe six feet two with a lot of muscle. A beer belly stands up front but if nothing else, the muscle on his arm and his weight alone could easily flatten Charlie. She's small, petite, and not made for this. I hope like hell they've trained her well enough. I doubt any of us want to see her pummelled. Although, I doubt it would ever get that far. I can't imagine Liam or Crow would allow a single punch to be thrown her way before they intercede. But then again, hopefully with what I've given Theo, any punch he throws shouldn't be too deadly or dangerous. He should be on his knees with just one punch once it kicks in.

The fight begins with Theo and Charlie inside the ring, circling one another. Theo is throwing a string of words her way that I frustratingly can't hear while Charlie looks completely unphased and remains silent as she eyes up her opponent.

Good, very good.

The tension building in the room is magnified by the silence that ensues. The room is eerily still as everyone waits for the first punch or kick to be thrown. There are bets made by everyone - on who will hit the other first, who will go down first, who will get back up, how long it will last, and if others will end up intervening. I didn't take part, but that doesn't mean that I'm not aware of them.

My phone vibrates in my pocket but I ignore it, knowing

that it will be one of my few very annoying friends wondering where I am. I had insisted that I wouldn't be coming tonight. Not only did I not want to see Charlie get inevitably hurt, but I also didn't want to cause a drama that wasn't needed, but I realised too late that I needed to be here for those exact reasons. I don't want to see her get hurt, but I can't stand to be away and hear about it without seeing it. I don't want to cause a drama and yet I am the first one to cause one by drugging Theo.

It isn't that I care about Charlie in the way I perhaps thought I did originally, but I do still care. A lot. She is one of the only people in my life that allows me to so freely be myself and I think I clung to that with everything I had when I first met her. She surprised me - astounded me even.

Theo throws his arms out with a fist towards Charlie that she narrowly avoids. The moment he throws the first punch, the noise in the room resumes. There's shouting, booing, screaming, and screeches coming from every direction. There are people cheering and throwing their hands up. Others are clapping while some are stood as stock still as I am while watching the fight unfold.

For too long, Theo throws punches and kicks that Charlie avoids as she practically and tactically chases him around the ring. It looks as though she's trying to exhaust him before she starts using her body against him, which is good. That's exactly what she should be doing.

What I don't anticipate is Theo catching Charlie, and yet he does. He manages to grab her ponytail, holds her still for just a millisecond as he throws a punch with all of his might straight into her face.

He lets her go and I watch with horror as she falls, crashing down, her head hitting the floor too quickly, and that's when absolute carnage ensues.

Crow's and Liam's eyes are filled with death wishes as they scramble to get inside, but what they don't see that I have the absolute glee of noticing is Charlie as she opens her eyes and looks up at Theo with a lethal danger and predatory fury unlike anything I've ever seen before. Theo isn't looking at her. His arms are in the air, rejoicing with what he assumes is his win.

The people surrounding the ring are too occupied to notice, but I do. I notice the smirk that lands on Charlie's face as a presence seems to consume her entirely. It's like watching a woman possessed as she lets her leg go out and trips Theo up. The shock on his face is beyond pleasurable to see as her men pause their attempts to get to her. Once they realise that she may indeed have the upper hand; a better chance than they originally assumed.

Theo falls heavily to the ground beside her, his eyes filled with confusion, but in less than a second, she's on top of him, throwing one punch after the other at his face, in motions so quick I can hardly keep track of her arms moving. She looks heaven made, God like, lethal as she descends her fists upon him. She looks like the most incredible monster I've ever seen, her eyes lighting up with the pain she's inflicting. Blood spurts out from Theo's face and covers her, but she doesn't stop. Doesn't hesitate. Doesn't slow. She pummels her fists into him until he's stopped moving completely, and then the smirk that covered her face returns as she slowly gets off him.

Crow and Liam, as well as everyone else around us, are deathly silent as they watch on. She stands above him, spits on his face, and walks around the ring, looking into the very soul of every person her eyes encounter.

"Now you fucking bow to me," she says, her voice travelling, loud and clear. I watch in awe as the people around us take her order very literally and begin getting down on their knees, smiles and roars once again filling the room as they cheer her on. Awe fills me as I replicate the actions of those around me and bow with a laugh nearly bursting out of me at the ludicrousness of the situation, watching as her eyes catch mine. Her lips twitch into a half smile as she nods my way, before Liam and her dad walk into the ring, holding one of her arms up each and announce her as the new President of The Dark Cobras.

The damn queen.

I glance once more at her brother that I know will haunt my thoughts before leaving the queen and her attentive bees to their business.

Twenty-Three

CHARLIE

The last time I was alone looking for Crow in this Clubhouse, I felt weak, afraid, and had a nightmare in store that I could never have anticipated but this time, as I look around for Crow, I have people nodding their heads, acknowledging me, I'm the President of the Dark Cobras.

"They're in Crow's room waiting for you," Gray whispers in my ear, his presence unexpected by my side as I look over at him.

"Why are they in there?" I ask.

Crow hasn't stayed in his room here at the club once since I've been home, and neither has Liam. Other than to pick up clothes or any other essentials, they've hardly left my side; I can't imagine why they'd be in there now.

"They've asked me to keep everyone away, to keep Dad distracted especially, so I'm going to guess that I don't want to know why they're in there waiting for you." He laughs lightly as he pushes me towards the hallway door.

The last time I walked down this hallway, I was out of my senses and alone. This time, I feel more powerful and majestic than I ever have in my life. I feel confident and like I could take on the world, and yet the niggling in the back of my mind won't leave me.

It doesn't take long to get to Crow's door. I stand, unsure of myself and what's waiting for me as my hand reaches for the handle. Anticipation runs through me as I open the door and find the absolute last thing I expected to see.

My heart soars, my body reacting immediately as I feel my core warm and my body shiver at the prospect of what's to come.

Liam and Crow on their knees, in only their boxers, their heads down. Waiting for me.

Their tattooed torsos and muscle-ridden biceps and chests while they kneel before me are inexplicably hot.

"Whatever you want, baby. We're all yours," Liam says as he looks up towards me, his eyes connecting with mine, his face filled with earnest caring and adoration as he waits for me to make my move.

Despite how powerful I feel in this moment, I want nothing more than for them to take me. To use me, to screw me and to make me feel nothing but them.

"Whatever I want?" I ask, curiously.

"Anything," Liam says as Crow looks up and nods at me.

"I want you both to ruin me. Make me yours, mark me, taunt me, please me. Do anything, I just need to be yours completely for tonight. I want you to take control."

Liam smirks while Crow's eyes go wide, always the more cautious of the two.

"Your wish is our command, baby girl," Liam says as he rises to his feet and strides towards me.

Crow's more hesitant but soon takes the hint and follows Liam's path to me. He stands back and watches for a moment as Liam undresses me. I'm suddenly glad that I took that shower after the fight. The last thing I needed right now was to be covered in blood and sweat.

Once I'm completely bare before them, Liam takes my hand and pulls me towards the bed, bending me over it. He falls to his knees again, the thud clear as the silence consumes me.

"Do you want pain?" Liam asks, his voice low and seductive as he speaks, his breath echoing along the insides of my thighs.

"Yes," I whisper, needing everything they can give me.

"Then stay still and count." It dawns on me instantly the memory of the last time he ordered me to count but unlike then, I am now completely in control despite our positions. I know that I can tell him to stop and he will. I can tell him to kneel or beg or jump from a damn plane and I know that he will.

"Make sure you're loud enough for me to hear." It's Crow this time that speaks, his low timber of a voice that penetrates me and makes me wet without a single touch.

I nod my head, words unable to form as I wait anxiously for his hands to land on me.

Only, what I expect doesn't come. What I find instead are lips on my inner thighs as he bites, over and over again, just hard enough for it to cause a bolt of pain and pleasure to run through me as Liam spanks my behind with his palm.

Crow's lips on me send shivers throughout my body, goosebumps all over me, my pussy wet and pleading for his touch. His lips hover over my clit and the lips of my core, just close enough for me to feel his breath on me, but he never dares to go further while Liam continues spanking me as I count loudly enough for them to hear me clearly.

"Are you ready for something special, baby?" Liam asks as Crow's mouth disappears from my body. I turn to find him standing again, his eyes not leaving the space between my open legs, his eyes filled with hunger and desire.

"I'm ready." I nod.

"Then get on your knees, baby girl. Let's see how much we can pack in your mouth."

I turn and get on my knees in front of them, realising that they both must have taken off their boxers without me noticing. They both stand completely naked in front of me, their cocks hard and pulsing in front of my face as I lick my lips.

"Just seeing you down there makes me want to fucking ruin you, princess," Crow says as he strokes his thick cock and presses the tip to my lips. I open for him immediately, taking him in completely, my eyes bugging and my throat tightening as he pushes himself all the way down my throat.

I suck and lick, the head of his cock hitting the back of my throat repeatedly as his head rears back, his hand in my hair while he controls our movements. My eyes flit between his and Liam's as I continue the repeated motion. Seeing him so turned on because of me makes me feel mighty and horny beyond belief.

"You ready to add another into the mix?" Liam rasps out as he takes his hand from his dick, his eyes hooked to mine. I nod, my mouth still full of Crow's pulsing cock.

Liam enters me alongside Crow, my jaw aching, my lips hurting and yet my core wetter now than it's ever been. My hand finds my clit, needing the tension and friction to help me. I find myself writhing and panting around their dicks as I do my best to take them in as far as I can. Their movements are identical as they pull on my hair, my scalp stinging from the motion.

The moans and noises escaping them send me into a fever as they fill my mouth, wanting nothing more than for them to fill me elsewhere.

"Is that your hand on what's ours, princess?" Crow asks, his eyes watching my hand.

I nod my head, just slightly.

"How about we do something about that?" he asks.

I nod again, my jaw and mouth sagging and panting as they take their cock away from me.

"Open her up, get her ready for us both," Liam commands, his order clearly intended for Crow who doesn't hesitate for a moment, his hands pushing me onto the bed, his face taking residence between my legs while his tongue and fingers immediately start ravishing me, stretching me and driving me wild. My hips lift and shake, my mind completely obsessed with the hands that are on me.

Crow's fingers slide in and out of both holes in a rhythm so quick that I can hardly comprehend it. My body moves and jolts with each movement, my eyes closing as I take in the overwhelming pleasure consuming me.

Hot lips, a wet tongue and rough hands encase my breasts and nipples, toying and taunting them tantalisingly slowly in comparison to Crow's speedy thrusts of his hands within me.

"You're so fucking wet, princess. You're such a fucking good girl," Crow utters before he very literally dives his head back between my legs, his tongue doing torturous things to me.

"I need you in me. Please," I beg, tears leaving my eyes at the all-consuming and unknown frustration and angst filling my body.

"Well, since you asked so nicely," Liam teases as he bites my nipple and makes a squeak escape me.

Liam and Crow seem to have an unspoken conversation, Liam nodding at Crow without any words spoken.

"Get up, baby girl. I want you on top of me."

I move to allow Liam to climb onto the bed beneath me, his cock protruding and filling my entrance. The immediate relief at having him fill me makes my body sag backward onto Crow just as he pushes me forward and coats my arse with lube.

"Fill her," Liam tells him. Crow takes the command and rolls with it, his hands pulling on my hair as he thrusts into me in one fluid and painful motion that halts my breath and fills me with a fire that I'm unsure will ever truly die down.

Within moments, I'm being moved and bounced on their cocks, feeling like I'm about to explode or be completely ripped apart and yet not wishing a second of it away as they use and ruin me just like I wanted.

"Fuck, your tits look fucking delicious like that," Liam utters as he holds my waist and moves me up and down, my breasts bouncing simultaneously with my body. He lifts himself up and grapples with my moving breasts, sucking a nipple into his mouth and holding on with his teeth as I move and thrust between them.

"You ready to cum, princess? Because I'm about to fucking break you," Crow whispers in my ear, his movements pausing, my arse so full of him that it feels impossible to think of anything else.

"Do it, please," I beg, needing everything and anything they'll give me.

"Don't say I didn't warn you." He chuckles lowly as he grabs hold of my throat, pulling me back towards him so that our bodies are flush up against one another. Crow behind me and Liam attached to my breasts, pounding into me from beneath.

And then he does exactly as he promised. He absolutely breaks me in two. He pounds into me in a quick, harsh, thorough succession while Liam holds me in place and moves me up and down his shaft.

I'm moaning and pleading in words that make no sense and mean nothing while they assault my every sense.

"Now cum, baby girl," Liam instructs as they both pound into me fluently and at identical moments, sending my mind and body to a place I've never dreamed of being, in some high up lost world only known for the strength of the orgasm that rips through me.

I feel both of their cocks pulse and release within me as I collapse onto Liam's chest, feeling completely and utterly ruined in the most earth-shattering way.

Crow rolls off me and lays next to Liam, pulling me between them. I curl into Crow's side, my head nestled on his chest while Liam spoons me from behind.

"Ruined enough for you?" Crow asks with a weak laugh as Liam brushes the hair from my face.

"Mhmm," I mumble and nod, feeling my eyes close.

"I've decided that I want revenge," I tell Crow and Liam. I mean, they're still sleeping but I'm practising telling them in Crow's bathroom mirror. Like any young woman does the night after becoming the President of a Motorcycle Club and having sex with two men. Right, so apparently I've not magically matured and gained a shit load of confidence overnight. Good to know.

I think back to the fight and the confidence and fury that felt like it was possessing me. I've never felt confidence or power like I did in that moment. I have no idea what made me say or do the things I did. Dad told me afterwards how much I'd shocked him and yet in all honesty, I think I had shocked myself as much as anyone else around me watching on as the power rushed to my head.

It was at that moment that I realised what I needed, what I craved. I craved very bloody vengeance. I enjoyed hurting Theo far more than I'd like to admit but I realised that it wasn't him I wanted to hurt as badly as I did, it was them.

I woke up about an hour ago and have been sitting on the floor of the bathroom for eighty percent of that time, thinking. Definitely over thinking, but thinking all the same. I feel like everything is finally starting to come together thanks to last night's victory. My dad, David, Crow and Liam, The Cobras. It all seems to be falling into place slowly. The only thing really holding me back from healing is my nerves, and the nerves only originate because I'm scared of Matt and Danny coming after me again, which means that I need to get my revenge. I need to see them bleed, and I need to make sure that they can never hurt me again.

That sounds logical, right? No, probably not, but I feel like it would make me feel better knowing that they're not in the world anymore. I know from what Gray and Liam told me that I'm far from the first person they've hurt, so I know that I'm doing what's right by the whole female population. I just feel like Crow and Liam might look at me differently if I tell them that I want to exact revenge on them. I have no idea why, I imagine they'd probably support me in it, but there's still a part of me that wonders if they think I'm going too far.

"What you doing in here? We snoring?" Crow asks me sleepily as he rubs his eyes and comes to sit next to me on the floor. He's got boxers on, but nothing else, and even that doesn't manage to distract me from my thoughts.

"Nah, just thinking," I utter.

"Penny for your thoughts."

"I'm not cheap. I want a pound," I tell him with a smile, watching as he gets up, goes back into the bedroom, and returns with a pound coin.

"One hundred pennies for your thoughts then," he tells me as he hands me the coin.

"I think I want revenge. I think that's the final thing I need to do before I can move on."

"Then let's go get ready to get your vengeance, princess," he says with ease as he stands and reaches for my hands, pulling me up with him and embracing me in his warm arms.

Twenty-Four

CHARLIE

"They're in there?" I ask Liam as I stare blankly at the door ahead. It's ordinary. Wooden. Nothing special. And yet inside of that door are the two men that set the whirling chaos in my mind in motion.

They are the ones that hurt me, scarred me, and rearranged my brain.

"They are." His words are heavy, his voice low, quiet.

The two guards outside of the door stare straight ahead, not looking at me even though I'm only mere feet away from them.

"You don't have to do this. We can take care of this for you, Char," Crow tells me as he brings his hand to the back of my neck and begins rubbing his hand back and forth.

I know I don't have to but I really, really fucking want to. They hurt me, and now it's my turn to hurt them. I'm feeling surprisingly strong but maybe that's because I haven't had to look at their faces yet.

"Are they healed from what you did?" I ask.

"Healed and tied up. They can't move," Liam tells me.

I nod. Good. That's good.

I walk forward with Crow and Liam to my rear and open the door, the guards not leaving their posts as I do.

They're each sat in a chair with a hospital gown, the only thing covering their bodies. They're facing me, the chairs around two or three feet apart from one another.

"Shut the door and tell the guards to come back later."

I'm not sure if it's Liam or Crow that listens to my command, but I hear hushed voices speak and the door close as I stand watching the fear filled faces of the imbeciles in front of me.

They're nothing. Ragged men probably not much older than I am, and yet they thought they had the right to touch me. To hurt me. To take what they wanted. But now it's my turn to take what I want.

Their manhood.

I twist the knife in my hand by its handle, my hands desperate to take action, but I remind myself of how I want this to happen. Slowly. I want them to feel the worry and terror that I did. I want them to see the blood and red and soaked skin that I did.

I walk towards Matt first and watch as he attempts to move away from me. His body can't do anything aside from sweat with the chains around his ankles, arms, and neck. The chair moves a little as he shoves his weight from one way to the other.

"Hold him." Crow and Liam take one side each, going to his back and holding him still.

The tape covering his mouth stops him from speaking but doesn't stop the noises that leave him as he attempts to speak or scream.

I've always thought of myself as a very empathetic individual but in this moment, I feel truly heartless. Psychotic. Uncaring.

I fall to my knees directly in front of Matt and lift the hospital gown up his legs until it reaches his waist. His penis hangs loosely between his legs as he attempts to shake his head, his eyes wide and terrified as tears begin to fall.

"That's right. Cry. Roar. Scream," I whisper to him as I look up into his eyes while a monstrous grin covers my face.

I take his flaccid penis in my left hand and begin severing it with the knife in my other hand. His movements and muffled screams do nothing but urge me on as I attempt to cut through the surprisingly tough skin and muscle. Blood squirts out and covers my face. I wipe the blood away from my eyes with my arm before continuing my pursuit, watching with keen curiosity as his eyes begin closing. His head lolls to the side as I finish the job I set out to do. The pouring blood doesn't stop as I finally slash the final piece of thin skin and take the severed skin and muscle in my hand.

It's tiny. Maybe an inch long. I'm not sure if it'll work for what I have planned. One can only try.

I stand and face who I now know is not Stoner but instead a man named Danny.

"Get me some more tape," I tell Crow as I look into his worried eyes.

In every other moment of my time with Crow and Liam, I've cared. Truly cared, but in this moment that I know will never leave my mind, I know that all I care for is getting revenge as I see fit.

This is my time. My decision. My right.

Liam leaves Matt passed out in his chair and follows me to Danny.

I rip the tape from his lips and spend a few seconds taking in his pleads.

"I'll do anything, anything you want. I'll do it myself; I'll chop it off myself. I'll never touch anyone ever again. I fucking swear, I swear." His begs and pleads continue until Crow reaches me with the tape I requested.

"Just cut enough off to cover his mouth again, please, and then wait." My voice sounds hollow and monstrous and yet I don't care.

"Stop talking or I'll make it worse for you," I tell the man in the chair. He immediately stops speaking, his eyes full of hope.

"You were inside of me. And now, he shall be inside of you. Open your mouth." I tell him as I feel an evil smile spread across my lips.

His eyes are as wide as saucers as he does the exact opposite of my order and closes his lips, jamming them shut.

A laugh bursts out of my lips as I watch his eyes soar between the three of us. No one is going to save him.

Crow and Liam may think of my tactics as wrong, sick, extreme, or fucked up and not one bit of me cares. This is my way.

"Hold his nose closed. He has to open his mouth to breathe at some point," I tell Liam, knowing that between him and Crow, he's the most accustomed and able to perform acts of violence.

Liam does as I say. I wait nearby with the bloody and useless muscle of penis in my hand.

It doesn't take long before Danny opens his mouth with a gasp. I don't miss my opportunity and shove the penis in his mouth before holding his jaw shut and telling Crow to tape his lips shut with the tape. He does.

And then I get back to work. I do the same to Danny as I did to Matt. Sever his manhood even though he's long since choked and passed out since then.

I take a step back and admire the work I've completed.

Only one more thing to do and then I can turn on the sane side of my brain and return home.

I look down at myself, seeing that the black leggings, black vest top, and navy zip hoodie are covered in blood.

"Are you done?" Crow asks.

"Nearly," I tell him as I smile, my sweet smile, the sane smile and take a step towards him.

I watch as Crow visibly gulps. He knows me well enough that I have no doubt he knows exactly what my plan entails from here. In order to remove and heal from memories, you have to replace them. And there's no one else I'd rather replace those sordid memories with than Crow and Liam.

"Our baby girl needs us. You can do that, can't you, man?" Liam asks with a sly grin thrown in Crow's direction.

I would never force him to do this if he didn't feel utterly comfortable doing so. So I watch Crow's face, searching for any signs that he's going to say yes and mean no.

He looks from me to Liam and then back to the now quiet men in the chairs beside us.

"Go and sit on his lap. Face me," Crow tells me, his words a command. An order. His face and eyes are filled with hunger and determination as he watches me sit on Matt's lap.

"Uh uh," Liam says with a shake of his head and a mock shake of his finger.

Crow and Liam look at one another before returning their gazes to me.

"Naked," Crow fills in for them both. They seem to have a connection whereby they can communicate without words - and I love it. I love that the men I love and need have as much of a connection with each other as I do with them. Admittedly in a very different way but even so.

I stand and take off my hoodie first, throwing it to the ground beside me, not phased in the slightest if it ends up dirty or covered in more blood. I then remove my vest, my bra, my leggings and underwear so that I'm completely bare before them.

"Now what?" I ask sweetly as I watch them stand beside one another and adoring the carnal attraction I have to them.

They're so different from one another and yet as I stand patiently waiting for my orders, I realise that I definitely have a type. Tall, tattooed, and deadly seems to sum it up.

"Go and sit on his lap again," Crow tells me.

I do as he says, feeling the still-spilling blood cover my bare behind as I sit on his lap.

He begins twitching as I do, the weight of me obviously waking him from his painful slumber. I pay no mind to him, his body beneath mine making me want to fidget and get out of the room, but determined to do what I set out to.

Liam is the first to come over to me. He falls to his knees and pulls my left breast into his mouth, sucking and laying light bites along the sensitive flesh.

Crow watches, his eyes alight as he takes in the scene in front of him.

"Aren't you joining us?" I wonder aloud breathlessly, the pleasure from Liam's lips, teeth, and tongue filling my every ending.

Crow's nefarious smile lights a furnace within me as he crouches down beside me, his hands immediately drifting to my entrance. I watch as his fingers use the blood covering me as lube while he enters me harshly with two fingers.

Liam's lips find my own just as a gasp escapes my lips and fills his.

Crow's fingers don't stop their insanely pleasurable assault on me, his thumb coursing along my clit as I hear the muffled moans enter my ears from the man beneath me. I pay no mind to him, giving Liam my all as his tongue darts out and fights with mine for dominance.

I realise too late that I'm grinding down on not only Crow's hand but the stub I left of the man beneath me. I don't want him feeling my pleasure, I decide.

I pull my lips from Liam's reluctantly. "I don't want to sit on him anymore," I tell them both and watch in awe as they say nothing but immediately take action. Crow takes his hands away from me, my insides feeling empty as soon as he does. He instead puts his face in place of his hand and then lifts me with his hands underneath my legs and reaching behind to my back to keep me upright. I look up to find that I'm very nearly touching the ceiling but feel incapable of concentrating on anything but Crow's head between my legs as he carries me so effortlessly above him while walking towards Danny.

"I don't want their bodies on mine," I whisper out, unsure of what Crow's plan is.

He adjusts his hands and my body, pulling me down so that I'm standing in front of them both.

"You aren't touching them. We are," Liam tells me huskily as he takes a seat on Danny's lap and pulls out his already hard cock, his hand sliding up and down the length.

I'm not touching them. They are, I repeat in my mind.

I go over to Liam and take his hand away, instead covering his length with my lips as I swiftly roll my tongue over the head of his cock and revel in the moan that leaves his lips.

I can feel Crow's presence behind me as he places his own dick at my entrance and impales me harshly, with so much force that it pushes me down further onto Liam's cock, the head of which now feels like its bulging out of my throat and yet as I look up with teary eyes from the sudden assault, the pleasure that fills me from Crow's continuous, rough thrusts and Liam's moans of pleasure taking over every sense I have. My hands on Liam's thighs help steady my body as I take and push back for more of Crow to fill me.

"Fuck, I need in her before I cum," Liam grunts out to Crow as he grips his hands through my hair and lifts my head off his stiff and leaking dick.

Crow leaves my body, much to my annoyance, leaving me cold and empty from the air around us taking his place.

Liam spins me around and pulls me towards his lap. I hear him spit in his hand before his fingers reach for my rear entrance as Crow's hands lift my legs so that they're held above his elbows. Liam lifts me in one swift motion and slowly puts me down onto his cock. The overwhelming sense of being so full halts my breathing for a moment as my arse adjusts to having his size and length filling me.

When I've had a moment to adjust and nod at Crow, he

brings himself closer and pushes his cock inside me once more. The immense elation taking over me ends abruptly when they both begin pumping in and out of me, seemingly perfectly in time with one another as I let go and allow my body to be moved and jolted by their movements, immersing myself in the euphoria soaring throughout me.

Crow's hand reaches for my neck, squeezing it to the point of pain at the same moment that Liam's hands begin playing with my nipples.

"Oh fuck," I breathe out, unable to keep quiet any longer as they continue to beat into my body in the best way imaginable.

"Cum for us, princess," Crow tells me as his eyes glaze over with hunger while he watches my breasts bounce up and down from their pumping actions within me.

"Be our good girl and scream. Let them hear you roar for us," Liam whispers in my ear as his hands grip my waist and pinch. The pain of his harsh grasp and Crow's hand on my throat has me doing just that and screaming out as an orgasm rips its way from my body.

Twenty-Five

CHARLIE

"Has he been acting weird to you?" I ask Crow as we leave the Clubhouse after my first official meeting as the President and head home.

"I don't think so. I mean, he's been a bit quieter than usual, but there's been a lot going on so I can't really blame him. It's a lot to process along with his own shit."

"Yeah, I suppose you're right." Liam has been off and when I say off, I can't exactly place what it is that's been off about him, but he just doesn't seem to be himself, which is worrying me.

He's had more trauma to work through than any of us. I'm on a waiting list to see a counsellor, and I tried to convince Liam to do the same, but he wouldn't. I'm not sure what it is, but there's something going on in his head that he won't tell me about and I hate it. If I don't know what's going on, how can I help him?

He'll be home soon; I can talk to him about it then. Dad has been at the Club more and more lately, to the point now that he's hardly ever at home. I think he's doing exactly what I advised to Gray by keeping himself and his mind busy and therefore not allowing the negativity to have time to fester.

It doesn't take us long before we're pulling up outside the

house. I go straight up to my bedroom to get dressed in something more comfortable and have a shower. My whole body is aching and although the shower helped, I can't help but feel so exhausted - mentally and physically, completely drained. I've been sleeping like the dead at night, and yet I'm still ready to have a mid-morning nap daily. It must be the chaos of everything going on.

As I leave the ensuite bathroom and walk into my room, I'm surprised to find Liam sitting on my bed, facing me with something silver and shiny in his hands. I can only see the end of whatever it is. It's small, and the way he's fidgeting with it in his hands makes me think he's nervous.

"Are you alright?" I wonder aloud as I begin drying myself off and getting dressed. His eyes don't leave the item in his hands once which considering I'm wearing nothing is rather surprising.

I pull leggings and a baggy top of Crow's on to cover myself before sitting next to him on the bed. Our thighs touch as I do, even through the clothes I feel his warmth.

I wait in silence for a moment, wanting him to know that he can talk and I'll listen. I watch him as his brows crease and he bites his lips uncomfortably.

"I've got something for you, but I want to say something first," he tells me, his eyes still downcast, not meeting my gaze.

"OK," I say, not wanting to spook or panic him by saying or asking too much when he's so clearly feeling anxious.

"I've been trying to be everything you need, but I know deep down that I'm too broken to be the man you deserve. I see so much of myself in Crow, and I realise that if I'd had the right kind of childhood then maybe I'd be able to be the sort of man that he is for you. I've done things to you that can never be forgiven, things that I can never tell you how sorry I am for. I feel like I can't live in a world like this when all that happens in my head is you. You and then the bad again. You're the only good in the dark, and yet even you aren't enough to make the darkness go away. I will never, ever be able to make things right between us, but I want you to always have a part of me, no matter what, so I thought I could get you something like Crow did. I found you the matching set so that no matter what happens in life, no matter where I go or where my mind takes me, you'll always have this because I know that no matter how complete you make me feel that I've been through too much to ever be whole for you."

He holds out his hand, a small silver key inside of it with the end containing parts of a story, just like Crow's necklace that currently hangs around my neck and yet, no matter the beauty and sincerity of his gesture, it's his words that cause the tears to leave my eyes and my arms to wrap around him as I nestle myself into his chest.

"You are more than enough, Liam. We're both a little broken and that's OK. We've got time to heal, time to get better. We can heal together," I insist as he sighs and wraps his arms around me.

He doesn't utter a sound for such a long time as he holds me. Feeling him breathe against me, his arms, his warmth, makes me feel both more alive and more fortunate than I have in a long time. Knowing how much he struggles and yet how much he fights that every single day to remain here with me is more than enough, more than I could ever express to him or make him truly believe.

He pulls back, his hands on my cheeks as he looks into my eyes with a vulnerable innocence that portrays his feelings in a way that no words ever could.

"You're so fucking perfect, you're practically blinding. I'll make it all better one day, I promise." His lips catch mine before I can respond, taking me off guard as he takes control, pulling my face towards his as his tongue skirts gently into my mouth. The dominance and soft touches are complete opposites, and yet utter perfection until he pulls away too quickly, leaving my lips feeling plump and pink from the sudden onslaught.

"You make everything better already." I smile up at him, knowing that he needs what I'm offering, even if it seems so slight to anyone else. To Liam, the smallest things mean the absolute world.

"Come on, we need to get going. Your dad's going to be back soon," he says as his usual smile reappears. He takes my hand and leads me to the stairs.

"Why do we have to go downstairs just because he'll be home soon?" I ask, unsure of the relationship between the two things.

"He's got your new leathers, girl. First woman to enter the Cobras and somehow ends up the boss at the same time. That's not bad going, baby," he says as he winks and drags me down the steps.

I hadn't even considered getting my own leathers, nor had I thought about how much that would mean. I'm not sure that I ever thought I'd want a set of my own but now that the prospect is being presented to me, I feel myself welling up at the truth of the responsibility and family that I've taken on.

"You alright there, baby?"

"Yeah, I'm fine, I just didn't expect to feel so emotional at getting my own leathers." I laugh lightly, feeling dizzy with excitement that I never anticipated that I'd experience.

I never thought I would even be a Cobra because of the rules surrounding women, or rather the lack of women on the Dark Cobras and yet, just like Liam said, here I am taking on the ultimate responsibility by not only being the first woman to join the Cobras but by being the President of them as well.

It's definitely time to make some changes.

Alice is my first call I note in my mind as I feel over the possibilities. She more than anyone deserves the title held with being a member of the Dark Cobras - if she wants it, that is. She's been there for everyone, through everything, despite her own tremendous battles and problems.

Liam watches me, his eyes inquisitive as I think over my potential plans for the future.

"You realise that you're doing that thing where you just freeze and think. You know you can sit down and think as well," Liam jokes while pulling me along towards the lounge.

"Yes, I know, I just didn't want to forget so I had to stand still to remember." I laugh as he sits next to me and pulls my legs over his, stroking his fingers along my thighs as he does.

"OK, well that sounds strange and like you have some memory problems. Is it time to see the doctor again?" he asks with a wink in my direction.

"Why's she seeing the doctor?" Crow has a mouthful of food as he speaks - ever the attractive gentleman, which means that his words come out more like a grumble of vowels and random syllables than an understandable set of words mashed together to make a sentence. I understand him all the same, but I still send him a roll of my eyes and a confused look.

"Are you ill?" he asks, stalling down the food and rushing over to me, feeling my head with the back of his hand and looking into my eyes.

"No, she's not ill, she just has a terrible memory," Liam tells him as he whacks his arm away from my head.

Crow throws a glare his way.

"You said doctor. I panicked. No one explained. What do you expect me to do?" He looks at Liam as though he's stupid and has completely lost his mind which just earns him a second set of eye rolls directed his way.

"Pretty sure that's your dad's bike out front," Crow says, completely unaware of what my dad's presence means as he nods his head in the direction of the window for me to see.

Twenty-Six

CHARLIE

"He hasn't replied to me at all," I tell Crow as he ushers me along towards Alice's door.

"He will. He's probably just having a mini breakdown and then he'll be back," he says nonchalantly.

I look at him incredulously. "That's not ok," I emphasise, wide eyed.

Crow does nothing but roll his eyes at me.

"He'll be fine. This is a lot for him. You know it is. There's no way he can just go from being his dad's slave to this and it not affect him, Char. You need to give him time. You know he'll come back to you, he fucking adores you," he says as we reach the door.

I take in his words, realising that he's right. Liam has never had anyone truly care for him aside from my dad and some of the Cobras and even then, he felt he had no choice but to sneak behind their backs to protect me. Of course, it would be a big deal. He needed time. I can do that. I just need to give him time. It will be fine.

I nod at him and knock on the door to Alice's flat, attempting to wipe my mind of any thoughts of Liam so that I could give my full attention to one of the only friends I have.

"They're here, they're here, they're here!" Kira squeals as she comes to the door and opens it with a wide smile on her face.

"Hey, Mini," Crow greets her as he ruffles her hair and steps inside.

"Alice is peeing but she said she'll be out soon," she tells me brightly as she closes the door behind us and tells us to sit down.

"I did not tell you to tell them I'm peeing, I said I was going to brush my teeth," Alice utters at her sister as she walks through from the bathroom.

"Where's Liam? He's my favourite," Kira says grumpily as she mock pouts and looks outside of the door again.

"Firstly, that's rude, little mini, I thought I was your favourite and secondly, he's having a magic moment where he disappears and then reappears, but he'll be back soon, little Haribo lady," Crow jokes as he takes a seat on the sofa, his legs spread wide as he invites me to sit between them. I shake my head, not wanting to be too physical in front of Alice and Kira, especially with what Alice is currently going through with Edgar.

"Fine, come here then," Crow says as he grabs my arms and yanks me down so that I fall right beside him, tucked into his arm as I do.

"People in love are so weird. Why do you touch each other so much? Makes me wanna hurl," Kira tells us, throwing her fingers down her throat and gagging as if to reinforce her point.

"You'll be in love one day too and then you'll eat your damn words, girl," Alice tells her as she walks into the kitchen and returns moments later with a tray of drinks.

"Can I tell you your future?" Kira asks excitedly, her eyes filled with wonder as she pulls out a tiny bottle of crystals and rocks from her pocket.

"Sure. What do you need me to do?" I ask with a laugh as I watch Alice shake her head and roll her eyes at her little sister's antics.

"Just put your hand out and keep it still," Kira says seriously as she shakes the bottle of rock in her hand and then tips them out onto my palm.

Her head dips, her eyes squinting as if to check the stones a little more and then looks at me, her eyes wide and curious.

"People are going to die."

My heart stops for a moment. Even though I know the likelihood of a thirteen-year-old girl telling me my fortune isn't going to be the thing to make her predictions come true, the crass mention of death has me feeling sinister and concerned.

"Jesus, Kira, what did I say about telling people fake and horrible fortunes?" Alice exclaims from her place in the kitchen.

"What? It's true, that's what it says!" Kira spurs back at her sister, picking up the rocks and crystals from my hand, pouring them back into the small container.

∼

"I think you've come on your period, princess," Crow says as he shakes me awake softly.

My eyes feel tired and groggy as I look around the bed, my mind not comprehending what it is he's saying.

"Come on, Char, let's get you in the bath."

I allow him to pull me up off the bed while still half asleep as I follow him into the bathroom. The bath is full with bubbles and my iPad on a tray, Netflix already on there, ready to play.

"You didn't just wake up?" My words sound slurred and sleepy as I speak.

"Nah, but I didn't want to wake you until I had a bath run," he says as he lifts his shirt over my head before he takes my underwear off and instructs me to try and go to the toilet while he turns around and then lifts me into the bath.

"I'm gonna go change the sheets and then I'll be back, alright? There's some water and chocolate behind your iPad too," he tells me with a sweet smile before kissing my forehead and leaving the room.

I nod and close my eyes as I feel the water cover me.

I take in the silence as I lay back and appreciate how lucky I am to have the likes of Crow in my life. I realise how often before I admitted my feelings for him that I wished for a partner similar to the men I read about in romance novels and yet Crow, with his ability to make me feel content, is more than anything I could have ever wished for.

His laughter, his energy, his kindness and thought is beyond anything I dreamed of when wishing for someone to love me because he does so much more than that. He doesn't just love me in the way that I do him, but he treasures and reassures me through simple acts rather than meaningless words without any need or want for reciprocation.

"Char." His voice sounds panicked and far away even though I see him right next to me as I open my eyes.

"You need to get out. Now." I look around, wondering what the problem is and come across it immediately. I can't have been in the water for more than a few minutes and yet the bubbles are nearly all gone and in their place is water that's turned red.

I've had plenty of baths while on my period before, but I have never experienced this.

"Crow, this isn't normal," I whisper as he gets a towel and carries me bridal style out of the bath, his clothes now soaked as I look up to see his worried face.

I get dressed and fill my underwear with more padding and sanitary equipment than is probably needed as Crow empties the bath.

The pain hits so suddenly that I find myself leaning over the bed in an attempt to ease it.

"Princess, you're leaking already."

"Matt! Matt, Gray! Fucking wake up, now!" Crow roars as he slams open my door and bangs on my dad's and Gray's doors before returning to me.

"I'm taking you to the hospital, baby. You're ok, everything's going to be ok." Only I suspect that both he and I know that nothing is ok because I think we both know what's happening.

∼

My bedroom doesn't feel familiar. Not the curtains or the bedding that Crow replaced only hours ago or the soft carpet beneath my bed. Not the ensuite or the wardrobe or the clothes inside of it. Nothing does. Not even Crow. Not my dad or the people that flock around me, whispering things to one another that they think I can't hear. I practically laugh at myself internally. I'm hilarious. I feel hollow and empty. They all seem to think I'm scared or upset or ashamed, but I'm none of those things. I'm nothing. I just am.

A knock echoes around the space surrounding me, leading my eyes to drift towards the door that slowly opens as Crow's head peeks around the side of it. My mind aches at the sight of him.

I see it in his eyes - the wishing for me to be me again. He doesn't say it or show it, but I know he must want me to just shake out of it. To go back to being me. He must. I do, so how can he not? I feel like the moment the bleeding started, the moment the doctor confirmed something so dreadful, was the same moment that I truly began to mourn - not just for the life leaving me but for it all.

"Can I come in?" he asks, his voice low and husky, still filled with sleep. He must be exhausted. He's been with me the whole time. Point blank refusing to leave. I haven't asked him to go but my dad has. Numerous times. Not because he doesn't want him here, I don't think it's him personally that he wants gone. I think he just believes that if things go back to normal or as normal as they once were that I will too. He keeps looking at me as if he doesn't know me. He looks as lost as I feel. I hate seeing him feeling anything other than himself.

I nod my head at Crow, letting him know that it's OK.

I smile weakly at him, and find myself staring at the wall above his head again as he kneels at the end of my bed.

"Do you want anything to drink or eat?"

"No, I'm OK, thanks," I tell him as I huddle into myself further, cringing as I feel myself bleeding again.

I can feel it leaking out of me. The blood. The life. Mine and its. The thing that was inside of me. The life that I didn't want but didn't have a choice in keeping or losing. The doctor said my body couldn't cope with the physical strain I was under and that was what they suspect caused the miscarriage. My body lost a baby. I'm losing a baby. A part of me.

They did a scan that made me sob the moment I looked at it. It was black and white and mine. And Liam's. I remembered that and sobbed even more. I thought for a moment that the universe was giving me something - something unwanted but still something of my own that would get me through the rest of my life, and then I remembered that he wasn't here, that I had no idea where he was, and that the blood meant that the universe was taking away the very thing it had gifted me. I hate that I don't have the choice to decide what I want to do. I hate that my body is taking that decision away from me. It feels like every choice I'm supposed to have in life is being and has always been taken away from me, and I'm not sure what choices I have left.

I'm not sure what I'm supposed to do now when I feel so little and so much all at once.

"Do you want to talk about it?" Crow asks gently, his voice barely above a whisper as he peers up at me huddled on top of my blanket.

"Talk about what? I don't know what to think, let alone know what to say," I tell him honestly, the exhaustion from my mind's exertion tiring my brain and body.

"Will you let me hold your hand? I just want to help you,

comfort you," he insists as his eyes widen and offer me more comfort than any physical touch could.

"Will you cuddle with me until I fall asleep, please?" I plead as my eyes fill with tears, blurring the vision of him in front of me.

"Oh Char." He sighs as he manoeuvres us so that I'm in his arms under the cover. "I'd cuddle you every damn moment of the day if you'd let me."

His arms immediately offer me comfort as I turn and sob in his arms, appreciating more than ever the soft touch he allows me.

His hands roam between my tangled hair and my back, rubbing gently along the clothes covering my skin.

He holds me until the sobs subside and sleep takes over, all while whispering the sweetest things in my ear.

"Did you know that a baby stays with you, is a part of you even after you've lost it? Alice told me that," he tells me softly.

"Did you know that you're the bravest person I know?" he whispers.

"I'll always be here princess. I'll always be by your side," he promises.

"You'll never lose me, you'll never lose Liam, and you'll never truly lose this part of you," he assures me.

"You'll never lose the baby because it will always be yours," he reassures as he strokes my hair.

"You'll always remember and so will I and so long as we remember then it's never truly lost," he tells me as I cry harder and harder in his arms.

"We'll plant a seed, let a tree grow, and watch as it blooms just like you and your baby would have," he says kindly as he wipes my tears away.

"We can bake a cake, throw a party, and decorate the tree as it grows every year," he decides.

"Just because you hadn't decided if you wanted it or not, that doesn't mean that it's any less yours or any less loved. You would have loved it and so would Liam and so would I. Any part of you would be adored and cherished."

"Thank you." My sobs subside while I cling to his chest, listening to his voice and appreciating his calming melody and his presence more than ever.

Twenty-Seven

CHARLIE

Crow's red Ferrari is waiting outside the house, but as I look inside for him, I notice that he's not there.

I pull my phone from my pocket with the aim of texting him, but at the very same instant, I feel arms lifting me from behind. I have a moment of panic before recognising the smell... Crow.

I spin in his arms, a smile appearing despite my mellow mood. It feels like one of those reunions you see online. The tear-soaked eyes, hugs that are never ending, and the light inside the eyes of the people reuniting. That's exactly how I feel. Like everything wrong is being lifted for just a moment as I wrap myself around Crow and squeeze him with every single bit of might I have inside of me. His arms are around my back, mine around his neck. He's lifted me so high that my head is above his and as he looks up at me as he slowly releases me down, I remember every single reason why he's both my best friend and everything more - because he makes me feel like this when it's the last way I think I deserve to feel.

I follow him to his car and find myself smiling again when he gives me a blanket to put over my lap and a hot water bottle for the pains that are slowly lessening.

Crow kept me smiling through times when I wasn't sure I wanted to even be alive. He protected me from my demons, made sacrifice after sacrifice to make me happy, and did everything imaginable to keep me going.

"How about we get some bad food for lunch?" he asks, looking at me with a nervous smile.

"You love bad food," he says as he continues driving onto the back alleys.

"Where are we going?" I ask, wondering why he's not going towards the main street where the usual restaurants and takeaway bars were located.

"Wherever you want, tell me what you want to eat, and we'll get it."

"No, I mean where are you heading right now?" I ask, confusion coating my question.

"Oh, I was gonna take you back to mine, but we'll get food first," he says as if it was that obvious.

Crow's hand reaches for my jaw with his eyes still on the road, and he squeezes.

"I can hear your teeth from here, woman. Stop it." I always do it when I am nervous or stressed or frustrated. My teeth start grinding, my jaw clenching, and he always knows whether he is looking or not, and he always holds my jaw tight as if it will solve the problem. It doesn't solve the bigger problem that is plaguing me, but it does immediately stop my teeth from chattering.

"You're an idiot," I say with a tight laugh.

"Yeah well, you'll be ugly and old with no teeth if you carry on that way, and we can't have that, can we?"

"You cheeky bastard!" I say, feeling a full belly laugh emptying its way from my mouth.

The guilt I feel for experiencing happiness as life escapes me haunts my mind. Crow and I spoke for hours upon hours last night and although logically, I know that I'm allowed to feel happiness, I also know that it will be a while before the happiness isn't plagued by guilt and sorrow.

"I'm trying to help you out here, Charl." He chuckles. "Do you want to be old, ugly, and lonely?"

"Oh, so I'll be lonely now too?" I ask. "And where might you be whilst I'm busy being a toothless old granny?"

His face lights up as he tells me, "I'll be out doing your shopping because you'll be too embarrassed to go anywhere in case you laugh too hard and your falsies fall out."

This is why Crow is and will always will be my best friend, no matter what else he is to me too.

"Oh, shut it. You're a prick," I tell him as I shove his arm just enough.

"Don't touch the jewels, love, don't touch the jewels," he says as he pulls away in mock pain.

"I'll be shovelling your damn jewels up your bleedin' arse if you carry on this way," I tell him with a glare. Not as though he sees it as he's too busy driving.

He pulls up outside of one of the most beautiful houses I've ever seen in what feels like seconds.

It's small and quaint, a cottage really, not a house. The walls are made of stone, different shapes and colours ranging the outside of the house, with vines and flowers flowing from the ground right to the tip of the tiles and slightly off kilter roof.

The garden is brimming with life and as I open the door to get out and look around, I notice a swing identical to the one I have at home painted in the most striking sunset orange that I've ever seen. It's my favourite colour, and I have a feeling Crow is well aware of that.

I turn to face him and find that he's watching me, waiting for my reaction.

"Is this place yours?" I ask in wonder.

"Something like that. I wanted to be in the city for such a long time, but I realised not so long ago that this was so much more beautiful," he tells me sombrely.

"It's incredible, Crow."

"You were the inspiration. You went on and on about your dream home often enough that you made your dream mine, and this is the result of that, so really, I've got you to thank."

I smile up at him, and rush over to the swing before plopping my bottom onto the cold surface.

Crow chuckles as he wanders over and takes a seat beside me.

"This is a home for all of us. I mean, I originally got it for you and me, but I've even added a shooting range for Liam." Hearing his words, his uncertainty about whether that will now happen crushes me.

I snuggle up to him, placing my arms around his back and his chest as he places his head on mine and whispers the words that he knows I love most in the world.

"Do you want some hash browns for dinner?" he asks.

"I'm not sure hash browns work for dinner. I'll put something together. Lead the way," I tell him as I elongate my arms in front of me.

I follow him up the cobble path as he leads me into the most beautiful entryway. It's like something from a film. The walls and decoration are all autumn shades. Yellows, oranges, purples, reds, and browns surround me.

As Crow shows me around, I'm taken aback by the natural beauty of the place. The inside is furnished with oak and it's breath-taking to say the least. It's a small, quaint place but it's so utterly beautiful that the size is just an added part of its charm.

"How did you have time to do this?" I ask in astonishment.

I turn to look at Crow and find him smiling mischievously at me.

"I started a few months ago when I bought the place. I knew you wanted to get away. Not far away, I know, but enough so that you had independence and a home you loved, so I've been working on it for us. When I wasn't looking for you, I was doing this," he says with a small, tense smile.

I swing my arms up and around him, squeezing him in ways that would surely suffocate anyone else, but has him only chuckling into my hair.

∼

"I take it this is the mighty Charlie Keller then?" a voice asks from behind me. I twist on the bar stool I'm sitting on in front of the breakfast bar to find a man I've never seen before.

He's tall with ice white hair sweeping across the top of his head and ridiculously bright, practically translucent green eyes.

"Oh, you alright, man? Yeah, this is Char. Char, meet Kenny. He's come to set up the security for the place."

Kenny. Kenny. Kenny.

"You called me a dick last time we spoke," Kenny tells me with a mischievous smile as he puts his hand out for me to shake.

"You were being a dick that night. Super unhelpful," I say pointedly as I shake his much larger hand. Firm, but not intimidatingly so handshake though. My dad would be impressed. He always used to tell me that I needed to improve my handshaking skills - as if that is even a thing.

"We're just heading off but you've got a key, haven't you?" Crow asks him as he rounds the table and helps me off the stool.

"Yeah, I'll be fine. I'll message you when I'm done. Nice meeting you, Miss Keller. A mini O'banian in the making, this one," he tells Crow with a nod in my direction.

"What do you mean?" he asks.

"She hasn't stopped glaring at me since I walked in." He laughs.

I have not been glaring at him, at least not on purpose. I'm pretty sure that's just my face. Oops.

"Sorry, I didn't mean to. It's nice to meet you too." I smile as Crow takes my hand, utters a few more words Kenny's way before he's taking me to his car out front.

"Do you think Liam will come back now? He's had long enough to think, right?" I ask as Crow begins driving off.

"Yeah, he'll be back, I'm sure o-fuck!" he exclaims as I feel the seat belt tighten around my chest and neck as the car jolts forward and stops abruptly.

"What the hell was that?" I mutter out, looking towards Crow as I notice a man pulling Crow's door open and grabbing him, pulling him out of the car.

By the time I take my seat belt off, there's a presence behind me and I know I'm done for. Again.

Twenty-Eight

CHARLIE

There's bad luck and then there's me it seems. Who manages to get taken twice in a short amount of time? Yep, that would be me, it seems, so as I sit up groggily on the surprisingly comfortable bed and look around the bare room, I wonder why the fuck I was taken this time.

My thoughts immediately run to Liam's father. Maybe Theo or Victor's father on behalf of Theo, though Victor had said that the two of them weren't particularly close. His father seemed more interested in the wellbeing of his club as a whole than the actions of an individual within it.

My body feels fine, other than half asleep. The pain in my stomach is still there though dulled by the magnitude of the situation that I am trying to play down in my mind in an attempt not to have a full-blown panic attack without anyone around and no idea where I am.

The bleeding is now lighter than it has been, which upsets me at just the thought that the loss is nearly over. I don't want the loss to last forever but knowing that I still have even just a small part of my baby inside of me fills with a strange sense of joy, but the bleeding stopping often means that it is coming to an end and that the baby, the foetus, the whatever you want to call it has left and I am alone again. Despite the fact that I wasn't aware I was pregnant, the thought of now being truly alone having lost the smallest thing that means the most absolute courses me. The door creaks open at that exact moment, and I realise that I don't have time to mourn. I only have time to do what needs to be done and, in this situation, that's working out who's taken me and form a plan to escape.

And yet as the man walks in, completely relaxed and calm, I realise that I am completely fucked because I don't need him to tell me who he is. I know exactly who he is because he looks identical to his son.

Liam's dad doesn't say a word as he enters the chamber and just watches me in silence for what feels like a lifetime.

"What do you want from me?" I ask, finally giving in after an eternity of his hard glare facing my direction.

"I took Liam and now he's here. I took you and now you're here. Your goal is to kill Liam and then I'll let you go. Simple." His voice is rough, low and commanding as he speaks.

"I'm not doing that," I insist with a voice that is nowhere near as confident as I hope it sounds.

"I thought you'd say that." He chuckles darkly.

"See, the thing is - if you don't do it, then my men, who thoroughly enjoy violence and men's weak spots will do it, and I can assure you that you doing it is a lot less painful and humiliating than them doing it."

∼

The walls are soundproof. No one will hear anything that I say. No one will know what I do. And now that he's sat in front of me on a metal chair with his hands tied behind his back and blindfolded, I find myself completely unaware of what to do or say. I can't do this. I can't let them hurt him but I can't not do this either. Seeing him like this takes me back to the events that unfolded that night with Matt and Danny.

I was sure that someone along the way would insist that I was demented, evil, and wrong for what I encouraged and did but in my mind, they deserved it. But this - Liam does not deserve this.

"I know it's you. I can feel you." His words stun me. He doesn't move, not as though I imagine he could move very much even if he wanted too.

I rush towards him and undo the blindfold from around his eyes, hating that his own flesh and blood could do this to him. The torture he'd been through his whole life was horrendous. The things he'd done and that had been done to him in the name of protecting others was unimaginable and even still, his life was a never-ending array of demonic torture and evil events - through no fault if his own. And now we are stuck. If I don't kill him, they will while making me watch, and I highly suspect that that won't just kill him. I have no doubt that they will drag it out. Hurt him. Maim him. Rape him. To hurt him as well as me.

"Are you here to kill me? I don't mind. I'd prefer my life be ended by your hand than theirs." He sounds confident somehow, even though his voice is hoarse and broken when he speaks. His words are emitting a confidence I'm sure he can't truly be feeling.

I don't speak. I don't respond, largely because I just don't know what to say or how to respond. I suddenly don't even know why I agreed. Except I do. Of course, I do.

"Let me hold you. Please. One last time," he begs, his eyes pleading with me. As if I could possibly say no.

My mind is still reeling and attempting to figure out an escape plan, but as I look around the nameless and empty room, there's nothing. No window, no vent, no way out.

I move to his back and use the knife they gave me to kill him to undo the ties holding him down. He waits patiently as I cut through the thick rope tying his hands together before rounding to his front letting my knees hit the concrete floor beneath him as I bend to cut the same rope from around his feet so that he's free.

My eyes stay downcast for what feels like an eternity, my heart racing as I attempt to compose myself and stop the incessant nagging in my brain. I realise now that I'm so close to him that he somehow still smells like him. Not like the alcohol that so often overpowered the senses like when I was a child but him. The man that I've grown to love in an entirely different way to what I thought I should. The same man that I know would conquer any army thrown his way to protect me.

I don't move as his hand drifts down to my chin and ever so gently places two fingers below it and lifts my tear-filled gaze to meet his.

"It's OK. I'm ready. I know what needs to be done. There's no way out of this, Charlie." I hate how accepting he is. I've never seen him give up or even give in to anything besides me. I don't want to see him give up now. I hate that he's accepted this lethal fate as if it means nothing. Maybe it doesn't. Not to him, but it does to me.

"Please don't cry, you know I hate it when you cry." His words are soft, low, quiet, barely spoken as I look into the forgiving eyes of the man before me.

His body looks stiff from being in such an awkward position for so long, but I soon realise that he must have saved strength somehow - somewhere, as he crouches down beside me, leaning back against the wall and pulls me onto his lap with what looks to take so little effort from him, my head against his chest while his chin rests on the top of my hair. I can feel his heart beating against my body, the steady thud thud thud that keeps mine from going into overdrive as I listen to his breathing and match mine to it.

"You're matching me again," he says with a sad laugh and a smile I can feel forming above me, one I have no doubt would wreck me if I saw.

"Will you say something please? I don't mind going, especially by your hand, but I just want something good before I go. Tell me anything," he insists, an order more than a question - one I'm willing to oblige as my heart shatters that tiny bit more every time he speaks.

I shift just enough to face him, seeing that his eyes are as glossed over as my own feel as he looks at me with his own screwed up version of love. No one else can see or understand it but I know it's the truth - that he does love me in the only way he knows how. It's the exact type of love I need though. No matter how misunderstood or strange it seems to others, it's his warped, overwhelming and all-consuming love that I've always longed for. I didn't realise until I was given the chance that I needed him. Him and Crow. My only constants. My every breath. My everything.

I swallow down the emotion clogging my throat as I decide to tell him the truth and a fact I've only now come to realise as more true than I knew it to be.

"Three things," I tell him, watching him as he intently watches me in return. "Firstly, you're not giving up. I don't understand why you're just allowing this to happen without even trying to get out but it's not... It's not happening and secondly, I need you, Liam. I thought you'd just left me," I cry out, my hands reaching for my eyes, rubbing the tears away as I continue, "I've been bleeding. Profusely. I thought it was just a heavy period, but Dad got the doctor out and it turns out that I was pregnant. I was pregnant, Liam. With what would have been your baby." I sob as I let out the words I'd been wishing to tell him since I found out.

His breath hitches at my words, his hand around my waist twisting and moving me until I'm straddling him, sitting atop his lap and looking directly at him as his eyebrows crease together and his face looks like it's about to shatter along with me.

"You had a miscarriage?" he asks, his eyes as haunted as his voice sounds while I numbly nod and grasp his hand in my own, intertwining our fingers together while he looks at me, eyes filled with more sorrow than I know what to do with.

"Did you know, that even after a loss, the babies DNA stays with you, as part of you forever?" he asks me, his free hand taking up residency in my hair as he softly runs his fingers through it.

"Alice told me that. I have no idea how or why she knew, but she did," I tell him with a nod.

"I'm so fucking sorry, baby," he cries, his eyes now streaming as he shakes his head and looks heavenward before returning his glassy eyes and tear-stained cheeks towards me. "Not just for that, but for everything. I'm so sorry that I'm so fucked in the head. I'm sorry that I've fucked you up just the same as me. I'm sorry that I took from you what wasn't mine to take. I'm sorry for everything," he tells me on a sob as his head falls and I instinctively catch it, holding his head against my chest this time, allowing him this moment to release it all on probably the only person in the world that cares and it's that thought and that thought alone that ruins me even further.

"You didn't. That's just it. You healed me, Liam. You and Crow have given me everything I never knew I needed or wanted, and that's why you can't let go now. Please, we just need to work together and we can figure this out. We always do," I insist.

Maybe I really am just so fucked in the head that I can't compute what happened and process it like a normal person would, but then I'm so grateful that I care for him the way that I do because despite what he's done and said and who he's been, I know that he deserves this. We deserve this. This moment - probably one of the only moments in his life aside from the time he's spent with Crow and I when someone has truly, with no ulterior motive, comforted and cared for him.

Liam lifts his head, his hands so gently holding my face as he searches my eyes.

"What was the third thing?" he asks, his voice that of a

broken man, which serves to tear me apart even further. All he needed was the right childhood, the right people to love and care for him and this could have been so different. This moment would never have come to be.

I watch him as I speak, taking in every emotion and facial movement he makes. "I forgive you. That's what you need, isn't it? That's what you need to stop this and try for me? I've seen you torture yourself for what you've done. I always thought me being with you was enough but it's not and that's OK because I forgive you. I thank you. I want you. I'm glad that you did what you did," I tell him lightly, the words barely above a whisper. I know he's heard though; I hear his breathing stop and sigh as he places his forehead against mine.

He moves his hands so that he has one behind me, keeping me steady and the other on my hand, my wrist, the one that I forgot was still holding the knife and the moment I look back into his eyes, I know what's coming.

"No, no, not yet. I can't do it, not yet. We can get out, Liam. We can get out," I rush out, my chest filling and feeling heavy as more tears shed from my eyes and I try to escape his grip on me. I move and shift my body, trying to fight his hold on me as he does what he sees as the inevitable.

"It's time now, baby, it's time to say goodbye," he tells me as he guides my hand and in turn the knife towards his chest with enough pressure that I feel his body's weak attempt to fight it before he gives in as he slowly presses the knife further into himself. I fight it, using my body and my hand in an attempt to stop it but even as I manage to pull myself away, I realise that it's too late. He's stabbed himself in the chest. His hand is on the knife. In my struggle to get away and stop him, he took the knife from me and did the job I'd been sent here to do himself - so that I didn't have to.

The blood is covering both of our hands as I reach for him and cry in his arms, his arms never leaving me.

"The next time our souls meet, I'll be a better man, I'll be what you need but right now I'm going to go and tell our baby how much we love them," he tells me in between his gasps for breath.

His face is becoming so pale as I try to pull the knife out from his grasp and chest and yet even with the pain he must be in, he still manages to stop me, to continue the murder of himself.

"I don't want you to go. I want you to stay," I tell him, my head shaking from one side to the other as I pull my hand away from the knife and the contact his calloused hand has with it as my eyes fill over and over again with tears that I don't even attempt to hide or keep inside.

"Will you stay until I go?" he rasps out, his eyes filled with a vulnerable hope I wish I could memorise and keep.

"Always." I nod, letting him put his arms around me one last time as I put my head against his chest and hold onto him with every bit of strength I have in the naive hope that some miracle will come and save him. Save me. Save us.

"I, I, ugh." I lift my head to look into his dimming eyes as he attempts to speak, his breathing becoming haphazard and uneven as the space around us becomes wet with his blood.

"I love you. Forever mine," he tells me as I watch his eyes dim and flutter closed for longer than I'd like.

"I know. I love you too." I have no idea if this was the moment I was waiting for, if fate knew that the words were needed now. I only know that it feels right at this moment to tell him. I know that he needs to hear it, and I need to be the one who says it.

I hold his face in my hands, bringing my tear covered wet lips to his in what I wish was a greeting but is instead a goodbye. I take in his last breath as I pull my lips away, watching his eyes take me in one last time before they close and his breathing halts completely, his eyes closing as my chest feels like it's being ripped apart, pressed down on and squeezed simultaneously.

I don't move from his lap, holding his hand and clinging to

his shirt as I pull his arms back around me, taking in the comfort he offers for what I know will be the last time as I sob into his still chest, missing the heartbeat that kept mine beating in sync from only moments ago.

He's not gone though. He's not gone. Not yet. No. He's not gone. Not yet.

I move his arms from around me and stand, adrenaline kicking in when I finally realise that in order to save him, I need to move. I check his breathing, thankful that although low and irregular that he is still breathing.

He's still here. He's not dead. Yet

I go to the door and bang, over and over again, shouting and screaming and willing my body to make as much noise as I can while pushing the weight of my body against the metal door frame with hopes that something may budge. Or if nothing else, that someone will get fed up and see what's going on.

What I didn't expect was to have the door open and find Crow standing there.

"Crow." My mind seems to blank at the reality of what's happening finally sinking in.

Liam is in a literal puddle of his own blood and Crow - somehow, by some miracle is here.

"I need help. He's got a knife wound. We need a doctor," I tell him as I rush back over to Liam, taking my hoodie off as I do and covering him with it.

"Get the doctor!" Crow yells out the door as he joins me and lifts Liam off the ground, cradling him like a baby.

They might have an unconventional relationship, but I know that Crow isn't wanting to save Liam just for my sake anymore. They've connected on more levels than I could have ever hoped for.

Twenty-Nine

CHARLIE

"You need to let go of his hand, princess. We need to get to your appointment. Your health is just as important as his," Crow tells me as I wish for a miracle and pray to a god I've never believed in.

Just let me be happy with them and I'll never ask for anything else again, I promise. Keep them both alive and happy and healthy. I promise not to ask for anything else. You can take me if you like, just don't take them. They deserve to live. To love. To heal.

I don't hear a voice or see a light, nor does any godly figure appear, and yet I hope that if anyone, someone or something is up there that they've heard my prayer and that I've done enough good in my life to have my prayer answered.

"Come on, Char. We need to go. We need to make sure you're ok." I let Crow guide me from the room, my hand in his as I curl up to his side, needing the closeness and comfort that him being near brings me.

I can't imagine a life without either of them. Without Liam or Crow. I know that one day I will be ok because that's what everyone says when someone dies. They say that one day, after years of healing, that you'll be ok but I don't want to be just

OK. I want to be whole. I want to be the version of me that I am when I'm with them both.

~

"That's not possible. I've been bleeding so heavily that.. that just can't be right," I tell the doctor sitting opposite me at his desk. He must have got it wrong. Even doctors get things wrong.

"I checked three times, I found the heartbeat. I would assume that you were pregnant with twins and lost one of them. I'm so sorry."

My eyes jump from one place to another, not truly seeing anything as my mind attempts to take in the words he is saying to me. That's not right. I would know if I was pregnant. I would know, wouldn't I? I would know that. Of course, I would. But then, I remind myself, I didn't have a clue until I started bleeding and saw a doctor to confirm something I had absolutely no clue about so maybe I wouldn't know at all.

The doctor slides a scan image towards me, his eyes and face gentle and unassuming as he watches me for a reaction.

"Is that the baby?" I ask, my voice sky high and yet quiet as can be as I stare at the darkened image with curiosity.

"It is. You're not too far along, so there's not much to see but I saw a steady heartbeat and right now, that's the main thing we need." His voice is gentle, as if he's afraid that I'm about to break, though that assumption may not be wrong.

I pick up the image in front of me and watch as the doctor points out what the different shaded areas are. He shows me the heartbeat, the baby. My baby.

I had completely forgotten that Crow was at my side until he places his hand on my thigh and gives me a reassuring smile.

"I'll give you both a moment alone," the doctor says kindly as he exits the room and leaves me stunned and unsure of what to say.

When the very same doctor confirmed the loss, I had

mourned. I had felt sorrow and sadness beyond measure. I hadn't even considered how I would have felt if I found out I was pregnant without the loss and yet here I am, my mind scattered and lost as I wonder how I'll cope. How I'll be as a mum. I'll be packing lunch boxes and school bags, getting them dressed and bathed, taking them on trips to the beach and hikes, and I have no idea what I'm supposed to do.

My whole world seems to freeze and turn on its axis, the future I had envisioned completely upturned and forgotten and yet there isn't any part of me that is saddened by that I realise as I look up to see Crow's tentative smile.

"I'll help you. I know you know that but whatever happens with Liam, I'll be there to help you both. You, him, and the baby. I'm not leaving you, Charlie, I never will," he promises me as a hand floats to my still pudgy but flat stomach. I am going to be round. Oh god.

"What are you thinking?" Crow asks me as I stare into the space between us, my eyes unfocused and as unsure as my mind is.

"I'm going to get round," I tell him simply, honestly, the first thought that enters my mind or rather the most recent one.

"I really don't think that's what you need to be worrying about." Crow chuckles as he takes the scan picture out of my hand and looks at it.

"That's your baby, princess. What if it's another princess? Shit, I'll never cope with two of you." He huffs out with mocking amazement coating his face.

"Oh, shut up, we don't even know yet. It might be a mini me and end up ruling the world."

Thirty

LIAM

My chest feels tight. As if it's wrapped in a bandage with a tonne of steel sat on me. I feel heavy and wonder why.

I force my eyes open and then it all comes back to me. My dad. Charlie. The knife.

Shit.

Well, I mean, I'm still here and that's got to count for something.

My eyes shoot down to the layers of dark hair on my lap. Charlie. Her face is turned in the other direction. I want to see her. I need to see her.

Fuck. I tried to make her kill me. I don't have much luck with women. I've never really tried to. I hadn't ever been interested in anything but a quick fuck before I saw Charlie as a woman for the first time. And then it all changed. And now I tried to make the one woman I had ever truly loved kill me.

Way to go, man. Way to fucking go.

And then I notice the hospital admittance band on her wrist and want to stab myself over again for leaving her and not finding another way out. The baby. The miscarriage.

My heart breaks more for her than myself, knowing that she's had to go through it all without me by her side.

I seriously need to see her face now. I need to know she's OK.

I lift my hand, which takes much more effort than I'd like, and place it on her head, my finger roaming through the loose and untidy curls. She stirs and pushes my hand away, which does nothing but force an abrupt and very rough sounding laugh out of me.

Charlie does not like to be woken up.

"Don't wake her yet." I didn't even notice that Crow was in here. I'd been so hyper focused on Charlie that I hadn't even thought to look around the room once she was in my view.

He looks as tired and worn out as I feel.

"Is she alright?" I ask, my voice quiet.

Crow raises a single eyebrow in my direction.

"She's fucking mad, dude and she's got every right to be. I'm pretty fucking angry at you myself as it happens," he hisses out as he leans towards me, his eyes filled with fury.

Oh, for fuck's sake. As if what I need right now is for them both to be pissed at me.

"I didn't think I had a choice," I tell him, knowing it's a lie and knowing damn well that he knows that too.

"Oh, fuck off with your bull, man. You were the one that put the fucking tracker in her. You knew that you could have halted the semi heroic, all together stupid suicide mission for a few more minutes and someone would be there."

We still hadn't told her that I'd done that. I did it the night before they'd come to get her from that hotel. God, it seems like a lifetime ago and yet like only yesterday too. How is that possible?

I hate even thinking about the things I'd done to her there, the positions I'd put her in all because I cared for her and my dad knew that she was my weakness.

"It's better for her if I'm not around. There's no danger then," I tell him, refusing to look at him as I speak, instead choosing to watch Charlie's still hair on my lap.

"He's dead. Your father. I killed him myself. Most of his band of bastards are dead too. No one's coming for you. Or her. You can be with us. She doesn't give a shit about what you did, and you damn well know it, now gather your fucking balls and be there."

He's young and yet wiser than I've ever been.

"Look, I'm sorry that you're mad I hurt her-"

"That's not why I'm pissed. Well, not all of it." He huffs out as he wipes his palms along his jeans.

"I'm fucking angry because you left us both. You promised both of us that you'd be there. You promised both of us a life and you fucking left. You left and let her try to kill you with no consideration for how the fuck it would leave us. She can't be with you without me, just like she can't be with me without you. I don't love you the way she does, but you're one of the only people I don't have to bullshit around so until both of us tell you to fuck off then you fucking stay put and pull your shit together. Got it?"

He's right. I know he's right and so does he. He's a cocky bastard, much like myself, and when I found that we actually got in better than I'd anticipated, I found something in him that I didn't want to let go of. Not a love like I had for Charlie but a bond, a connection, a friendship that I knew would last. I just didn't realise that he felt the same way.

"Alright, enough with this sappy shit. Can I wake her up now?" I ask as I cover the shake in my voice with a cough that just about kills my damn lungs.

Rule one after a self-inflicted stab wound to the chest - Do not cough.

"Go on then. Her mood's on you though," he tells me with a sigh as he sits back in the chair and watches on with keen interest - probably wondering how I'm going to go about waking her without getting a fist to the face.

"Charlie, you gonna wake up, baby?" I ask as I stroke her hair, willing her to wake up so I don't have to go any longer without seeing the face that keeps me sane.

She fidgets a little, a small and weak groan escaping her lips, but shows no sign of waking.

"Baby, wake up," I tell her again, this time allowing my voice to be an octave lower and louder.

And then she does wake and true to form, she whacks me right in the ribs, sending a shooting pain through me.

"Fuck," I hiss out as I lean forward in the bed and grab my middle.

"Oh shit, I'm so so-" she starts but stops herself. "I'm not even sorry. What the fuck was that?" she inquires, her words striking me.

"Me waking you up?" I ask gingerly.

"No, not you waking me up. What was that? Crow told me about the tracker." I find myself eyeing Crow up. He lifts his hands in surrender as if to say what do you expect, dude? "You tried to kill yourself, you stupid fucking bastard! You're lucky you're in a hospital bed, or I'd bloody whack you again," she says as she scrunches her nose and brows together, appearing frustrated and annoyed, but I know she's not, or at least not as much as she probably wishes she was.

The tears fill her eyes within seconds before she rushes to me and falls in my arms. It takes an enormous amount of effort to shift my body and wrap my arms around her but like fuck am I doing anything besides comforting her in this moment.

"I'm sorry," I whisper, meaning the words but feeling nothing short of ecstatic - taking pleasure in having her so close. Her scent draws me in, makes me feel at home as I feel her soft body against mine. The pain it causes is practically numb, no pain being worth thinking about while having her here with me.

"Do you remember what I said? About forgiving you? Because I do. I really, really do," she quivers out, her sobs racking my chest both physically and mentally and fucking ripping me apart.

"I know. I'm sorry, I just.. need to do better," I tell her. I know I need to overcome some of the shit I've done and that's been done to me, but I also know that until I've done that, I'm not the man I need to be for her and since I can't imagine a time that I'll ever be able to leave her side, I guess being better is what has to be done.

She lifts her tear-stained face up to look at me, her soft eyes all-consuming and mighty in their stead.

"I don't want you to be anything other than you, Liam. We can work the rest out together. Crow's the least traumatised, well - we've probably traumatised him ourselves at this stage, but he can be the sane one, OK? Right, Crow?" she asks him with a ridiculous innocence covering her face as she looks over to him hopefully.

He rolls his eyes and laughs. "Yep, that's me. Protector of the traumatised," he says as he puts his hand over his heart and bows mockingly before saluting us both.

"See?" Charlie says, her face beaming.

I wouldn't ever admit it, but I dreamt of having someone that gave me everything as a kid. Before I knew how fucked the world was, I dreamt of having someone care for me and now that I have it, there's not a fucking chance in hell I'm letting it go.

"Yeah, yeah, I see," I tell her with a small smile.

"Oh, and one more thing," she says as she sits up on her chair nervously, her hands leaving my body.

"Don't pout," she orders me. I didn't realise I was, though considering she stopped touching me, I'm not surprised to find my automatic reaction is to act like a stroppy toddler.

"Anyway, so, I had to have a scan last night to make sure that everything was.. gone," she stutters, "and well, it's not.

They think it must have been twins and that I lost one because there's still one healthy baby. I'm still pregnant."

My eyes shift between her nervous smile and Crow's cocky and laughable one as I take in what she's said.

Well, fuck.

The dream fades as quickly as it came, the black scenery in front of my eyes taking over again as the vision leaves my mind.

"I'll protect her, I promise you." It's Crow's voice. I can't see him, but I can hear him. His voice is thick with emotion.

I think about his words. I don't trust him with my life, but I trust him with hers. Above anyone else, I trust him.

This is it. I could feel my body failing, my mind short circuiting as sobs fell on my ears and soft hands touch the hands I can't move. I wish I could comfort her. I wish I could be for her what she needs but instead, my eyes won't open and my body won't move.

"Tell them we love them. We'll wait for you, OK? We'll-" The sobs start again, her voice breaking.

I'm so sorry, baby girl.

"We'll see you again. We'll come together again in another life when we're all better. I'll find you; I promise." Charlie. Charlie. Charlie. I need to find Charlie. I need to find our baby.

Charlie.

The beeping signalling my heart rate stops and turns into a continuous open ending ringing.

Charlie. NO.

∼

Charlie

I've never experienced grief before. Not really, not like this. It feels like I'm experiencing grief for more than just myself. I'm grieving for the baby inside of me that will never know their father. I'm grieving for Liam, for the person he could have been with the right help. I'm grieving for my dad, who despite the obstacles they've been through, has lost a lifelong friend. I'm grieving for Crow who has to watch me in despair. I grieve for myself and everything that the three of us could have been.

But the worst part of all is that I have no idea how I'm supposed to let go of his hand that is only getting colder and stiffer. The nurses and doctors don't rush me. They don't ask me to leave or beg me to stop crying and wailing like I'm losing my own life. They don't tell me to get it together. They also don't tell me how quickly death changes a person. Liam's eyes are closed, his life having left his body. The shell of him that's left here is nothing more than a body, and yet it's the very body that deserves so much more than it was ever given.

I don't speak as Crow tells me that they're all dead. Liam's father. His father's men. The ones that took us. No one is coming for me anymore, which only makes it worse because if he'd lived, if he'd just kept breathing, if he'd just believed for a little longer that he was worthy and loved and cared for, the three of us could have lived a life together. It may not have been perfect, but it would have been ours.

I watch from the sidelines as so many people come and wish him the best in his new life, wherever that may be. I watch as they whisper what I assume are kind words or goodbyes. I watch in horror as Crow takes my hand and pulls me closer to Liam's side. I watch as he lifts Liam's hands and places it on my stomach. On our baby. I watch as his face contorts when I sob and cry and wonder why life is so cruel.

I watch as they take his body away. I experience the grief, the guilt, and the loss over and over again for what feels like a lifetime.

I spend an eternity praying to Liam, asking him to watch over our baby in Heaven while I watch over the one that will soon be on Earth. I promise him every night in my dreams that we'll meet again. We'll be better the next time we meet. Our souls won't know pain or depression or torture or trauma. I promise him that the three of us will live together one day with our children. One day, we'll sit together and watch our children play as the love between our souls passes through the world we reside in.

I tell him good night; I tell him that I love him and that I'll see him again one day as my heart breaks and Crow attempts to fix it in time for my baby's arrival.

～

"Do you think he can see us?" I ask, my voice betraying me. I had hoped that I could come here and not cry but it seems impossible, especially with Eli in my arms.

I look up at Crow from my spot on the floor. I feel closer to him this way. On my knees, knowing I'm above him. Just a few feet away. It sounds morbid and somewhat demented, but looking at the gravestone in front of me makes me feel like I can feel him. Hear him.

Crow rocks Eli gently in his arms, his soft snores the only noise around us aside from the whistling birds and rustling trees.

"I think he's watching you. Watching Eli. Probably watching me too," he says with a laugh as Eli snuggles further into Crow's chest.

"He'd be proud of you, Char. You know that." He whispers so as not to wake Eli from his slumber. It seems his hushed words don't work though, for Eli's eyes start to peel open.

"Hey, baby boy," I coo as I take him gently from Crow's embrace.

"This is your daddy," I tell him with a sniffle as I edge closer to the gravestone residing in front of me.

The flowers around it need replacing. I've been coming to see him every few days since we laid him to rest but hadn't been for nearly a week since I had given birth.

It still hurts to be in the position I am - on my knees but it is the only way I feel close enough to Liam not to sob.

"He was kind and brave and-"

"And crazy," Crow interrupts with a playful smile.

"And a teeny tiny bit crazy," I add on with a small laugh as I look down into the mirror image of Liam's eyes.

"But he would have done anything to protect you both. He might not be here but I have no doubt that he'll protect you still. Come on, the weather's cooling, we need to get you both inside," Crow tells me as he ushers us up from the ground.

I take one last look at Liam's name on the stone, reminding myself to breathe as my chest tightens.

"You've got Eli and you've got me. You've got Liam watching you and one day, we'll see him again. You've got everything you need." Crow repeats the words he's said a million times since Liam passed away. I nod my head, knowing he's right.

I take Crow's hand in my free hand and continue to rock a curious-eyed Eli as we walk back to the house.

I insisted on having Liam buried in the garden of the house Crow prepared for us so that he is always close. So that we can all see him as often as we need, whenever we need. I've spent more nights out here with Crow by my side than I have inside of the house, but as time goes on, the visits become less frequent. From spending every waking moment next to him to now seeing him every few days.

I knew that one day, whether that be before or after my death, that I'll find him again. I'll have him and Crow by my side once more. The next time I have them both, I will never let them go.

But for now, Crow and I settle into a healthy pace and a lifestyle filled with bustling busy bodies keeping us occupied. We live a peaceful life with me studying from home while feeding Eli in a rocking chair with Crow watching diligently by my side.

Liam may be Eli's father but until he's returned to us, Crow vowed to help me raise Eli as his own. He adores and cherishes him more than any man I've ever seen. He is truly besotted which fuels the love I have for him even further.

Liam will look after and love our baby in Heaven while Crow and I will love the baby we have on Earth.

Thirty-One

CHARLIE - 5 YEARS LATER

"Eli and Grace are officially with your brother and his lover. Does this mean I get my lover all to myself for a little while?" Crow asks mischievously as he wraps his arms around my swollen and pregnant belly from behind. Even after all this time, his touch sends butterflies somersaulting through my stomach. His baby also happens to be doing somersaults in there right now as well.

"Well, I was going to catch up on the washing," I tease as I continue to fold Eli's school shirt and place it on top of his pile of clothes.

We've set a list of chores for Eli now that he is a little older - one of which is taking his clean clothes up to his room, and yet I already know that it will end up being me doing it again. He has the most mischievous glint in his eyes every single time when he begins fluttering his lashes and telling me how tired he is, so of course he can't do it. I am the sucker that gives in nearly every time though.

"Have you seen yourself? All I have to do is look at you and I'm practically covering the place in cum, it won't take long," he whines mockingly as his hands begin to caress my breasts rhythmically.

"I suppose I can take a five-minute break," I tease with a smile as I turn and wrap my arms around the back of his neck and press light kisses along his stubbled jaw.

"Nuh uh," he says as he pulls back and wags his finger at me with a smile.

Shit, he's so beautiful. He's aged and grown more handsome over the years.

"If you start touching me, I'm not even gonna get inside of you before my load busts everywhere like some horny teenager," he says as he pulls me along to the lounge, sits on the sofa, and places me down so that I'm straddling him.

My dress rises enough that it's surrounding my waist, just under my bump.

"You're not wearing any underwear?" He hisses as his fingers find my clit and begin strumming away delicately, igniting a fever pitch of need within me. I always need him, want him, but pregnancy and a bit of a beard on him sets me in a frenzy. Even more so than usual.

"I had a feeling you might want easy access." I smile as I layer my lips along his neck and lift myself up so that he can get his thick cock out of the material currently restricting it.

The head of his cock bumps along my entrance, agonisingly slowly as he pulls the top of my dress down and begins nibbling and nipping at my breasts.

"Oh God, just put it in, Crow." I pant as he chuckles sexily.

"So impatient, princess. Say please," he says as his hand holds his cock just out of reach.

I look down into his hunger filled eyes and beg. Happily.

"Please. Please fuck me, Crow," I beg breathlessly and smile as he grunts and fills me in one swift motion.

He holds my hips and meets my every thrust in his direction as I lift and dip my body over his continuously, loving the feeling of being so full of him. Every time he is inside of me, it makes me feel like I am about to be ripped open. His size is otherworldly and yet I crave nothing more than to be completely and utterly ruined by him.

His roar of desire meets my moans as he ravages my neck with his mouth, my head back to give him access.

"Oh fuck, baby, you're so fucking perfect," he praises me as the pressure within me builds to unimaginable heights.

"I'm gonna fill you and then fuck you again. I can't get enough of you. You make me fucking ravenous." He groans as he grabs the back of my neck and meets me in the middle for an agonisingly slow kiss, the pressure on my neck firing cylinders within me that set my orgasm alight along with his fingers at my core, pressing and squeezing teasingly.

He empties his load in me, his warm cum squirting inside of me as I fall onto him, my head on his shoulder as he strokes my long hair gently.

"I love you so fucking much, Char," he beats out breathlessly in my ear.

"I love you too," I say as the world goes dark for a moment and I feel myself begin to drift off. I love falling asleep with him still inside of me. He's convinced it's why I ended up pregnant so quickly when we finally decided to start trying to conceive.

"Come on, let's go find the kids and your brother and his lover before you fall asleep again," he tells me.

This pregnancy has taken the energy right out of me. I seem to sleep more than breathe at this stage. I'm always falling asleep in the middle of the day, finding Eli or Grace stroking my cheek and shouting for Crow once they notice I'm asleep.

Eli is the sweetest soul. He noticed that I fell asleep last night while watching a film and lay next to me, stroking my hair and pulling a blanket over us both. Grace, being so young, doesn't understand the element of silence that's needed to sleep so she often shouts for her daddy to be quiet and wakes me in the process, but I don't mind. Not in the slightest.

Being able to live and love the life that I have while still dealing with a rendered heartache is the most I could ever wish for.

I pull myself off of Crow, clean myself up in the downstairs bathroom, and rearrange my now creased dress as we leave the front door and head to the meadow where the children are bound to be with Liam's grave.

We set the kids' play equipment and toys up right next to it, which Gray told me was morbid as hell, but they both love it. Eli knows that Liam is his father. He talks to him daily, even though he calls Crow his dad too. Grace isn't that great at talking yet, but even she babbles along and brings Liam and Eli flowers while they're talking.

It might not be the most conventional dynamic, but I don't want Eli to feel like he didn't get the chance to know his dad even though that's exactly what happened. I want him to know him through us, but I want him to feel like he can talk to him himself anytime he wants to as well.

It doesn't take long to find them all. Eli is playing football with Gray and his lover, as Crow so eloquently puts it, while Grace is tiring out said lover by making him chase her around the garden. I find my smile lifting as I watch the scene in front of me with Crow's hand in my own.

Life is full of the most horrendous heartaches, and yet I'm simultaneously bombarded with the most sensational love and happiness in the simplest of things and for that, I have no doubt I have Liam and my baby in Heaven to thank for watching over us and keeping us content and happy until we can see them again one day.

But until then, I plan to spend every moment of the life I have, living for those that I have with me as well as for the ones I'm without.

"You're still a shithead!" Crow shouts at the man on the field as Gray gives him the stink eye for cursing out his boyfriend and Grace copies before giving said shithead a hug and babbling something his way.

Eli drags me towards Liam's grave and tells me that Liam wants to play a game. Crow soon joins in with Grace and with our family so close to being complete, even without all of us earth-side, I thank every and anyone that's ever listened to my prayers.

Thirty-Two

DIARY ENTRY

My dream has always been to write. To write a story that changes minds, confounds readers, and sets dreams alight. I just didn't think this would be the story I would tell.

For the second and last time, I'm signing this for you. For him. For everything we never got to be.

In another world, we'll have it all.

I'll see you again one day, but until then, I'll raise our son to be as mighty and wonderful as you were both always supposed to be.

Until we meet again.

Signed For Him. For You. For Us.

Charlie Keller (give our baby a kiss from me!)

Contact Me

If you enjoyed the Signed with Love Duet, I hope you'll be pleased to know that Gray's story is next! You can pre-order on Amazon: Sign The Line (Book 3)

I also have a readers group that you can join on Facebook called J.R Dusts Book Besties that we'd love to have you join!

You can follow me on:
TikTok
Instagram
Facebook
Goodreads
Or email me at j.rdust_author@yahoo.com

Acknowledgments

There are so many people I'd like to thank for helping me bring this story to life!

My editor (Magnolia Editing Services), my proofreader, my lovely PA Amanda Johnson as well as my cover designer and the designer that creates all of my beautiful teasers (forgetyounot.designs).

I also have the most amazing team of Beta and ARC readers that have become more than just readers but really close friends as well. They are constantly hyping me up, supporting me, and encouraging me and for that, I cannot thank them enough! It truly means the absolute world to me.

I'd also love to mention my family for always supporting me with my writing and just life in general! My mum for reading my books, my youngest sister for letting me talk about them non-stop, my partner for being the most incredible person I could have ever wished for, and my babies for being the best little humans in the world (yes, I'm biased but they totally are!) I am so grateful and thankful to have such amazing people around me.

And lastly, to those of you that have taken the time and the leap of faith with the Signed with Love Duet: I appreciate you endlessly!

Printed in Great Britain
by Amazon